Song
Hunter

Also by Sally Prue

Cold Tom
Ice Maiden

'The Truth Sayer' sequence
The Truth Sayer
March of the Owlmen
Plague of Mondays

Song
Hunter

Sally Prue

OXFORD
UNIVERSITY PRESS

OXFORD

UNIVERSITY PRESS

Great Clarendon Street, Oxford OX2 6DP

Oxford University Press is a department of the University of Oxford.
It furthers the University's objective of excellence in research, scholarship,
and education by publishing worldwide in

Oxford New York

Auckland Cape Town Dar es Salaam Hong Kong Karachi
Kuala Lumpur Madrid Melbourne Mexico City Nairobi
New Delhi Shanghai Taipei Toronto

With offices in

Argentina Austria Brazil Chile Czech Republic France Greece
Guatemala Hungary Italy Japan Poland Portugal Singapore
South Korea Switzerland Thailand Turkey Ukraine Vietnam

Oxford is a registered trade mark of Oxford University Press
in the UK and in certain other countries

British Library Cataloguing in Publication Data

Data available

ISBN: 978-0-19-275711-1
1 3 5 7 9 10 8 6 4 2

Printed in Great Britain
Paper used in the production of this book is a natural,
recyclable product made from wood grown in sustainable forests.
The manufacturing process conforms to the environmental
regulations of the country of origin.

To Elizabeth Roy

The events in this book take place about forty thousand years ago, in a time when mammoths could walk across the area now covered by the North Sea, and the people were of the kind we now call Neanderthals.

Chapter 1

It was coming. The blustering wind was covering up the sound of the beast's great feet, but the whole valley had begun to shudder with fear. With dread.

Mica tightened her grip on her axe. The flint edge was sharp, but the creature's flesh was so thick that her blade would do no more than enrage it, turn it to the attack. And a single swipe of its—

There! A shrill whistle: and there, over on the other side of the track, a sharp *tk!* in reply.

Mica shifted cautiously as she crouched amongst the long tufts of grass. Those sounds had not been made by birds, but by stonemen. The beast must be very close, now. The whistle had been Elk's order: *be ready*, and the tongue-click had been Seal's answer.

This was the hardest part of any hunt. All Mica had to do was keep absolutely still and silent while the others chivvied the beast past her and on towards the bog—but still Mica's heart was thumping in her chest.

The stonemen had surrounded the beast with small sounds: soft whistles, or tiny squeaks, or sudden rustlings in the wind-swayed grass. They had to make the beast just uneasy enough to turn aside from its course and pace quietly on towards what it thought was safety.

There was a great huffing snort from a little way down the track. It was so close Mica nearly bolted. She wanted to run so much that she had to clench her fist round her axe to stop herself doing it.

But it was all right. Of course it was. The beast was close, but it didn't even know she was there.

Mica discovered she was shaking. This creature was so dangerous.

That was partly the reason for the hunt, of course. Elk was the Strongest of the stonemen, their chief. Getting them to kill the biggest beast they'd ever seen would prove yet again his right to be leader.

And that was why all the stonemen (except Pearl, who was too old, and Lynx, who had been born only six seasons ago) were hiding out here amongst the long grass of the snow-scabbed hillside, waiting and waiting for the terrifying moment when—

There was a sudden screeching bellow from right above her and Mica forgot everything. She pushed herself to her feet and there, in one confused, horrified moment, she saw it all.

It was so huge. So *huge*! It filled half the sky. And then faster than thought (that was the most terrifying thing, faster than *thought*) it was lashing out with its great trunk, and Seal was having to throw himself out of its way to avoid a bone-splintering blow.

Mica had never seen a beast like this so close. Nothing like this close. She could smell its rage, see the glint of its small eye, hear its coarse hair rustling in the wind.

She wanted to run, but the sight of the beast's power took all her strength away from her. She stood in full sight and gaped at it.

A mammoth. A mighty bull mammoth, close enough to—

—but now Seal had scrambled up again and he and Elk were charging towards the beast. They were bellowing, thumping their wide chests, brandishing their spears. Bear was there too, waving his arms and roaring in his new deep voice. Behind the great bulk of the beast Garnet's and Amber's voices were cutting the air, high and sharp like the cries of hawks.

Mica needed to run. Needed to run. Needed to run: but she couldn't take her eyes off the great towering bulk of the mammoth. Even Elk, even *Elk*, seemed tiny beside it.

Garnet was running screeching into the path of the beast. It saw her and swerved, and then it was running, too, straight towards Mica: and though Mica tried to move, tried to throw herself aside, her legs refused to obey her.

There were shouts from all round:

'*Mica!*'

'*Mica, run!*'

But Mica's body was frozen, and—

'*Mica!*'

Bear was charging towards her through the rough grass, and the sight of his horror-filled face made Mica's mind suddenly snap clear.

Run. *Run!*

She turned, got somehow caught up in a clump of grass and all at once she was rolling, rolling, with the sky and earth tumbling round her.

And suddenly the huge bulk of the beast was above her, blotting out the sun. Somewhere someone was shouting something but she couldn't tell what it was.

This must be the end. It must be. Any moment now it would trample her, crush her bones.

Despite her terror Mica somehow got to her feet again. She held up her flint axe in both hands and screamed out a shrill and desperate defiance.

But she was hardly more than a gnat to it. It swiped her out of its way with its trunk and Mica went flying.

Mid-flight, the sun went out.

Chapter 2

Mica opened her eyes and found she was outside on the hills. She was lying twisted awkwardly through the tussocks of the wind-whipped grass. Her head was thudding horribly. What on earth . . .

The mammoth! It had been right above her, and then . . .

The valley was quiet, now, except for the murmur of busy voices, and the sound of axes slicing through flesh.

A shape appeared against the pearly sky above her.

'Are you all right?' asked Bear, anxiously.

Mica wasn't sure. She tried to sit up, but the movement sent the snow-scraped hills lurching so violently round her that she wouldn't have made it if Bear hadn't caught hold of her arm to steady her.

Bear's hand was filthy with scabs of dark blood. Yes, the stink of blood was everywhere. The breeze was thick with it.

Mica looked round and there was the mammoth, just a handful of paces away. It was dead, surrounded by ice-splinters and half sunken into the reed-pierced bog.

So they'd killed it. The stonemen had stampeded it into the mire and then speared it while it was panicking and floundering and sinking into the mud.

They'd killed it!

Elk and the others were busy round its body. There was need for haste because the stench of blood would soon attract hyenas and lions. There was meat enough in this great corpse to feed all the beasts of the valley, of course, but only a fool argued with a lion if he could help it.

In any case, winter was coming and the stonemen needed every scrap of meat they could get if they were going to survive to see the spring.

Mica let Bear help her to her feet. The corpse of the mammoth looked mountainous, even half sunk into the bog. Mica shivered at the sight of it.

'We nearly lost it,' Bear told her. 'It was headed off up the slope, but you turned it aside just at the last moment.'

'Did Elk spear it?' The first spear-thrust was Elk's duty because he was the leader of the stonemen, their Strongest.

Bear hesitated.

'I stabbed its eye, first,' he said, blushing a little.

Mica stared at him.

'You . . .'

'Well, it was near getting out of the bog.'

'But how on earth . . . '

'I stepped up on its tusk. Got hold of its ear. Stabbed it with my axe.'

Mica gaped at him. The thought of Bear jumping up onto that great roaring, lashing creature. Of grabbing hold of its flapping ear . . .

'That was crazy, Bear,' she said, at last.

He shrugged, frowning.

'The others finished it off,' he said. 'Mica—'

But Mica had just realized something else. Bear had struck the first blow. So that meant the mammoth was Bear's kill.

She looked at him.

'You are grown-up,' she said, really shocked at the thought.

He blushed even more deeply.

'I only stabbed its eye. I don't know if that will count.'

But of course it would count. Of course it would. So that meant Bear was grown-up. Mica could hardly believe it. They'd been friends forever: but now Bear was grown-up and that meant everything would be different.

'Mica,' said Bear, 'there's something else. The mammoth—it fought back. Both spears were broken.'

Mica forgot all about Bear's being grown-up: she went cold with horror.

'*Both*? Broken badly?'

'One halfway along. The other in three pieces.'

But their spears were vital. The river brought them

pieces of wood quite often, but seldom anything long enough or straight enough to make a spear.

'But how will we hunt without spears?' she asked, stupidly.

Bear pulled his heavy wolf-pelt up over his shoulder. The bindings that held them in place had come loose in the hunt.

'We'll have to hide in the grass and hope some beasts come along,' he said, unhappily. 'We have our axes.'

But that was ridiculous. No good at all. Their spears were vital. *Vital*. There were eight mouths to feed, and winter was coming, and they weren't going to be able to kill anything of any size with a hand-axe. You'd be taking your life in your hands trying to kill even a *horse* with a hand-axe.

Down by the edge of the bog Elk was hard at work slitting his way into the mammoth's hump. The hump would be full of fat, valuable for both eating and fuel. The beast's trunk had already been cut off and lay ready to drag back to the shelter, and now Seal and Garnet were hacking with their hand-axes at one of the beast's great legs. The meat from a mammoth's leg was almost as good to eat as the trunk, though it would take all Seal's great strength to drag the thing home.

Elk beckoned to her, his eyes bright under his brow-ridge. His face was shining with mammoth grease and the joy of the kill.

'Come, then! Come, Mica, if you're all in one piece!

We must be busy. We don't want hyenas to get this, do we. *Or* those sneaking lions.'

We must be busy was Elk's motto, and of course he was right. Here was meat, and winter was on its way, and the leaves of the little birch shrubs had long whirled up into the cloudy sky. Even if their spears had not been broken, every mouthful of meat would have been very precious.

Mica clambered cautiously over the partly submerged corpse of the great beast. She settled her axe in her hand, pulled the beast's long hair out of the way, and began to hack as hard as she could at its other foreleg.

Chapter 3

A head of white hair shone through the dusk of the clearing as Mica made her way heavily up the track to the shelter. Pearl's eyes were milky with age, but her hearing was still very sharp.

'Mica?'

'Yes, old one.'

'They killed the mammoth, then. I heard the beast's death-call.'

'Yes, old one,' said Mica, putting down the great piece of meat she was carrying. 'It was a great bull.'

Pearl's mouth worked busily, as if she were chewing a piece of gristle. She often did that when she was thinking, even though she didn't actually have any teeth left to chew anything.

'And now you've come for fire to keep off the fanged ones,' she said.

'Yes, old one.'

Pearl nodded, pleased to have worked it out.

Mica went and got a bundle of fat-dipped rushes and lowered one end carefully into the embers of Pearl's fire. The torch would smoulder quietly for a long time, but it would flame up fiercely if it was whirled around.

Lions and hyenas hated fire. Hated it. It was only the stonemen who loved it, who tended it, who had it for their slave.

'Can I come with you?' asked Lynx, popping up at her elbow. 'I've been really good all day. I've turned over a whole pile of dung while you've been gone.'

'Well, all right,' said Mica. 'But you'll have to stay close to me because the smell of that mammoth'll bring every fanged beast in the valley this way.'

'Did Elk and Seal spear it?'

'Of course they did. But Bear got in first with his axe. So he's grown-up, now.'

'Really? Oh, I wish I'd seen it! When I'm grown-up I'm going to spear a mammoth every day. Rarrgh! Rarrgh! Take that! And that!'

He ran off round the clearing, stabbing invisible spears into invisible beasts. But Pearl's milky eyes stayed fixed on Mica.

'Something is wrong,' she said, accusingly.

Mica hadn't wanted to be the one to break the news, but she should have known there was never any chance of hiding anything from Pearl.

'Both the spears got broken,' Mica said.

'What? Both?'

Pearl hunched her thin shoulders and began to rock backwards and forwards as she sat.

'Then how will the stonemen hunt?' she muttered. 'Oh, the fool had to go after a great mammoth, didn't he. And now we'll all be bones before the spring. Oh yes. You mark my words.'

Mica glanced over at Lynx, but he was still running about pretending to spear mammoths.

'You'll frighten Lynx,' she told Pearl.

Pearl snorted.

'Lynx is too young to believe in death,' she said darkly.

Lynx ran back to them. He was jumping with excitement.

'Come on,' he said. 'I want to frighten a lion. Quick, Mica. Come on!'

Pearl waved them away with a wrinkled hand.

'Yes, go,' she said. 'The stonemen need you to watch their backs. But keep one eye on that young one, Mica, he is too young to understand what he should fear.'

Mica led Lynx back towards the bog where the mammoth's corpse lay. They'd stand up on the slope while the others dragged the great hunks of meat home. A fully-grown stoneman could face off a lion, but even Elk was vulnerable to a stealthy attack from behind.

The wind was vicious up here, laying the grass flat against the ground with every gust, and every puddle was scummed with ice. Mica pulled up her furs round her neck. Pearl insisted that the winters were getting colder year by year, even though the very mention of the idea was enough to send Seal into a rage, shouting and pointing and stamping his feet.

Mica did not like Seal much, but she thought he must be right about the cold. Surely nothing as huge as the turning of the seasons could ever change.

'Mica!' yelled Lynx, excitedly. 'Look! *Look!*'

It was a lion sure enough, and a dangerously mangy-looking one too. Luckily it was heading for the corpse of the mammoth, and not for the group of blood-bespattered stonemen who were dragging great joints of meat back towards the shelter.

Mica shook all thoughts of the earth's seasons out of her mind.

The stonemen could not afford for her to lose concentration for a moment.

Chapter 4

The stonemen sat around the little dung fire in the dusk, belching gently and picking at their teeth. They had brought home as much meat as they could carry, and they had fed themselves well.

An oozing chunk of mammoth flesh sat beside the fire, still slightly warm with its living blood.

Pearl nudged Mica, who leant forward to slash off a large piece with her axe.

'Don't you swallow that,' said Pearl, darkly.

Mica shook her head. It was her job to chew Pearl's food for her. It took so long to get the stuff into a state where Pearl could swallow it that Amber worried that Mica wasn't getting enough to eat herself. Mica was ridiculously skinny and small-muscled compared with the other stonemen, who were short-limbed and round-chested; though Mica could run fast and far if she had to, so you couldn't call her feeble.

'Time for some broth, wife,' said Elk, with great satisfaction, rubbing his hands together.

There was a mixture of meat and water all ready in a piece of rawhide that was supported inside a ring of stones. Amber took up an antler and used it to pick up a hot stone from the ashes of the fire.

Mica laid a hand on Pearl's arm, and the old woman turned her head to receive a wodge of chewed meat. Pearl champed at it noisily as Amber dropped the hot stone into the water.

The stone hissed violently as it touched the water, and the broth shifted, bubbled, and began to steam.

Everyone took in deep blissful breaths as the scent of the broth rose into the air. Then Garnet gave her son Lynx a sharp poke, and he remembered his manners and passed the shell of a river mussel to their Strongest, who always ate first.

But Elk shook his great head. He nodded to Bear.

'Your kill,' he said. 'It was your kill, Bear. You are grown-up. You are man, now. Today you have first broth.'

Bear ducked his head, blushing. But then he took the shell and dipped it into the muddy meaty warmth of the water, smiling and smiling, and looked as if he might swell to the size of a woolly rhino with pride.

The broth was eaten at last, and its warmth was lying comfortingly in the stonemen's bellies. Lynx had fallen asleep against Amber's shoulder, and Pearl was busily scraping out the bottom of the broth-hide. The fire had died down to embers. The noisy flapping of the wind-tugged hides that formed the door of the shelter behind them only served to heighten the contrast between their full bellies and the bleak hillside beyond the clearing.

'When we wake we must bring back all the meat left on the carcass,' said Elk, at last.

'And the grass from its belly, too,' agreed Pearl, baring her empty gums in a grin of pleasure. 'Delicious! That'll put hair on your chest, Bear!'

Seal's black eyes were glittering through the twilight. He was always quick to resent attention being given to anyone except himself, or his wife Garnet, or his son Lynx.

'It will take more than mammoth grass to make Bear a proper man,' he said, with scorn. 'Bear has struck first-blow, but he is far from having the strength of a grown stoneman.'

Garnet nodded her agreement (she always agreed with everything Seal said) but Bear looked across at Elk.

'True,' said Elk, unperturbed. 'Bear is a man because he has struck first-blow, but he is not man-strong yet. But that will come soon enough.'

'I doubt it will be soon,' said Seal, dismissively. 'And even if it does, what use will it be now we have no spear for him? We should never have hunted the mammoth. It's likely to be the end of us all.'

Mica held her breath. This was only a minor disagreement, but it was only a small step from a disagreement to a quarrel.

And one day a quarrel was going to lead to disaster. One day Seal was going to challenge Elk to a fight to prove who was strongest, who should be leader of the Men.

Amber spoke hastily to fill the gap where anger might begin to grow between the two full-grown men.

'We need to gather the mammoth's brains tomorrow, too, as well as the grass from its belly,' she said. 'We have three deer hides ready to be scraped and we have barely enough brains to cure them.'

And at that Elk nodded his foxy head, quite cheerful again, and began to give out orders for the next day.

Once the last spark of the fire had died the stonemen retreated to the pitch blackness of the shelter, wrapping their furs round them for the night. When Mica felt a pair of arms slip round her waist she thought it was Amber; but then the smell of wolfskin told her it was someone else.

Bear was warm, but for the first time ever it felt uncomfortable to have him so close.

'It's time to sleep,' she said quickly.

Bear's whisper tickled her ear.

'I'm grown-up, now,' he said. 'Just think, Mica. I killed the mammoth, and so I'm grown-up. Everything's going to be so different. There's all sorts of things I must do now I'm a grown man.'

Mica batted his hands away impatiently.

'Well, in that case you'd better go away and sleep, and hope you get hairier in the night,' she said.

Bear let go of her at once and went quietly away to his place between Pearl and Lynx.

Mica was very tired, but she still lay for a long time staring up at the dark roof of the shelter above her before she could get to sleep.

So much had changed since just that morning. Bear had grown up, and so their friendship was bound to be different, now.

And their spears were broken.

Chapter 5

The days after a big kill were always frantically busy, and now their spears were broken it was even more vitally important that they made the most of every scrap of meat. As much of the meat as possible had to be cut into thin slices and hung on reeds to dry (scaring off the crows and kites was Lynx's job) and all the meat that couldn't be dried had to be cut into chunks and thrown into the pond. This meat was sour when it came to be eaten, but it didn't usually poison people, or grow maggots, in the way meat left out in the open did.

The hide of the mammoth was too thick and heavy to be much use for anything, but the hair made excellent bedding, or stuffing for the hides the stonemen wrapped round their feet.

Mica spent the morning slicing mammoth meat, and then in the afternoon Elk sent her down to the bog to scoop out the mammoth's brains.

The wind was bitter again, but Mica was careful to push back her furs before she started to cut her way into the mammoth's skull through its eye-socket. It'd take hours for fur to dry out in this weather—and that was if it didn't simply freeze solid on her arms and flay the skin off her.

Luckily Seal's wife Garnet cared nothing for the cold. She squatted on the mammoth's shoulder, stocky, sour-faced and powerful, with her thin hair whipping round her in rat-tails, and hacked her way into the beast's great belly to retrieve what the hyenas had left of its liver and heart. Seal and Bear were busy cutting off great quivering lumps of valuable fat.

'Do you need any help?' Bear kept coming to ask Mica in breaks to stretch his legs.

Mica and Bear had always worked together a lot, and it was good that he still wanted to help her even now he was grown-up. It wasn't a sign that he was being patronizing. No, of course he wasn't. But even so . . .

'I'm only scooping brains,' she couldn't help pointing out, on the third occasion he came over. 'I'm not trying to carry the whole beast home by myself, Bear!'

But Bear only smiled gently, pushed back his dead-grass hair with the back of a filthy hand, and went back to his work.

Elk spent the day trotting backwards and forwards between the shelter and the carcass, providing encouragement or orders or muscle-power, as necessary.

This mammoth would keep the stonemen fed for two moons at the least. That meant, as Mica was sure they'd all separately worked out, the mammoth meat would run out during the very darkest days of winter. The stonemen needed to kill a lot more beasts if they were going to live to see the herds of deer and horse return in the spring, and without spears Mica had no idea how they were going to be able to do it.

But despite this the stonemen's hearts couldn't help but lift at the sight of all this meat. Even Seal's grim expression relaxed a little as he cut expertly along the icy veins of fat. If the stonemen had full bellies, and shelter, and furs to bind round them, then they asked for nothing more.

To be fair, Mica wasn't sure herself what else anyone could want. But still, recently she kept finding herself filled with a deep longing for . . . for *something*, though she didn't know what it was.

She'd tried to explain this to the others, but Pearl had only nodded, and said:

'Bear will help with that,' and made the others laugh.

But it wasn't Bear Mica wanted. She was very fond of Bear, of course she was. Bear was kind and strong, and a brave hunter, and they'd been best friends almost for ever. But what she wanted . . . what she wanted was as fragile and translucent as the air, and as impossible to grasp.

There was a sudden buffet of wind that sent her ducking down against the scab-edged hide of the mammoth. This was not any time or place for daydreaming. A mammoth kept its brains right at the back of its skull, and her whole arm was slimy and raw and bitterly cold. They needed these brains quite as much as the beast's meat, though: if there were no brains then the stonemen could cure no hides, and without hides they would freeze to death in a single night.

Mica sighed. Sometimes she couldn't help wondering what the point of being alive was, if all her life was endless drudgery.

'Do you need any help?'

Bear again. His face was glowing with health and the vicious wind.

'No,' said Mica, a little shortly, because she couldn't help but suspect that Bear was taking this *grown-up* thing just a bit too seriously. But then a mixture of guilt and affection made her say: 'I've nearly finished, Bear.'

A call from up the slope interrupted anything else Bear might have been going to say.

'All well, young ones?'

That was Elk trotting along, hurrying as usual, his huge nose billowing out huge clouds of steam as he went. He'd already travelled from the mammoth corpse to the shelter and back several times that day.

Of course, what Elk was really saying was *there's much too much work to do to waste time talking*.

'I've got that leg finished, Strongest,' reported Bear, abashed.

'Good, good, good. Good, Bear. Then we'll see to the belly, now. Oh, and Mica, Pearl needs you back at the shelter if you've finished with those brains.'

Mica grasped the corners of the hide which held the frogspawn-mass of brains and began to lug it back towards the shelter.

None of the other stonemen seemed to notice the *endlessness* of all this work. Of all this trying to stay alive. Even Bear didn't.

But then Bear was naturally hard-working and contented, and he'd never given anyone a moment's worry ever since he'd arrived at the shelter. That was one of Mica's first memories. She'd run out to meet Elk, and for once he couldn't pick her up and swing her round because holding tightly on to one of his huge hands was a very small Bear.

Elk had found Bear sitting on the corpse of a great black bear over on one of the hills where the stonemen hardly ever hunted. Bear had been quite alone. He hadn't been crying, or hurt, but he'd gone with Elk quite readily.

How a child of three seasons had managed to kill a bear single-handed no one had ever been able to imagine.

In any case, Bear had lived happily with Elk and Amber and Mica and Pearl and Garnet. Seal had arrived one stormy spring evening a season or so later. Bear and Mica had been the only young ones in the band until Lynx had come along, and so of course they'd been best friends. And they still *were* best friends: they'd shared everything, absolutely everything, until recently Mica had begun to want something . . .

. . . but there she was again. Yearning for something. Not Bear, not food, nor shelter, warmth, companionship nor even love. Something that she had no name for.

Something . . .

. . . something impossible.

Chapter 6

Mica lay gasping on her grass bed. Her heart was thumping hard in her chest, but it was all right, it was all right, it'd been only a dream. There was no angry mammoth about to crush her.

So it was all right.

Just beyond Mica's feet the hide door of the shelter was flapping and cracking, but it was well weighed down and the air inside the shelter was fuggy with the presence of bodies and breathing.

At least two of the stonemen were snoring, and between the snores Mica could hear the blubbery bubbling of Pearl's slack lips.

Mica gritted her teeth. Tomorrow was going to be a busy day (like yesterday, and the day before that, and the day before that. She spent every day hunting and working and hunting and working and . . .) and she needed to rest.

But before Mica had even begun to feel sleepy a new noise had started up from somewhere outside in the darkness. It was an odd sound, a bit like a howl, or perhaps a little like the call of a bird, except that it wasn't nearly so high and it went on and on and *on*.

Mica groaned to herself. How was she going to get to sleep *now?*

The hide door suddenly gave an extra loud rattle as if some invisible hand had shaken it; but that was only the wind, of course: outside the valley would be shuddering in the bitter night.

The strange howling sound wasn't showing any signs of stopping. Mica could hear it clearly over the snuffling and scratching and snoring of the others. She'd been hearing sounds like it for a couple of moons, on and off, but had never known what to make of it.

In some odd way these howling calls were as much like a stream's voice as a bird's. Yes, they were a bit like ripples, swaying and rocking, as a young one is rocked to sleep—though the last thing those calls were doing was lulling Mica to sleep. They weren't the slightest bit peaceful or restful. They were lilting one moment, and startling the next; rising to shrillness, and then floating down to a bee-sweet humming; they were truly exciting, though in ways that Mica couldn't begin to understand.

What *were* they? It would be no good asking the others, because the stonemen neither knew nor cared about anything unless they could eat it or use it. Mica had long since learned that.

'It's nothing,' Pearl would say, spitting disgustedly, even if Mica had brought a shell worn pale and luminous as the moon to show her.

But how *could* it be *nothing* if Mica could hold it in her hand?

Mica had at last come to understand that asking questions about mysterious things like icicles, and voices in the night, was wrong. Questions just made the stonemen baffled and uneasy.

Even Bear wasn't interested. Not really. He was always too busy collecting fuel for the fire, or helping with the hunt. Bear loved all that. He would shake his head at Mica's questions. Even Elk treated them as jokes.

Not one of the stonemen ever seemed to wonder why the sky glowed like a fire in the evening, or where the wind came from. The glow and the wind were there—and then they were gone, gone, and it seemed to be only Mica who noticed the bouncing of the warmth-tinged fretful grass.

Mica could still hear those long howling calls. They weren't very loud, but they rose and fell like the hills, full of . . . full of . . . but she needed more words to describe them, and they did not exist.

Mica got up suddenly, pulling her fur cover round her, and carefully tugged the door-hide free of the rocks which held it closed.

The air in the clearing outside was cold enough to tingle the inside of her nose.

Above her the moon was floating, sharp as ice in the star-speckled sky. Mica took a step forward into the darkness. All she could hear now was the ceaseless whispering of the grass and the thudding of her heart, but then the calling came again: quite low (it was almost as if the valley itself had found a voice, she thought) and warm, somehow, like new-shed blood. And there, there it was again. Not far away at all. If she took a few steps across the clearing then surely . . .

Silence again, now, but around her the darkness had suddenly become alive with . . . with *something*. Mica went forward a few more cautious steps. She hadn't tied on her foot-hides, and her feet were already numb with cold.

And there! There, behind her, gushing into her mind so that for a moment the clearing seemed to flare with fire.

Mica spun on her heel and saw something, or only just missed seeing something, it was hard to be sure which. There was certainly a shadow, or a movement: something dark amidst the greater darkness. Something which wasn't blown aside by the wind.

She took three quick steps towards it—

—and walked straight into something solid.

She opened her mouth to scream, but the scent she took in with the breath told her what it was.

'Bear,' she said, flatly. And at once all the fear and wonder went out of the night.

She could only just see his outline, but somehow she could tell he was smiling.

'I woke up and you were gone,' he said simply. 'So I came to make sure you were all right.'

Mica sighed to herself. It was practically impossible to be really annoyed with Bear.

'There was something out here,' she said.

'And you went out after it?' he said, admiringly.

'It was making strange noises,' said Mica. 'It was like—'

But then Bear suddenly gripped her arm.

'You're right,' he whispered. 'Did you hear that rustling? Over there. Hey, and I think I can see it, too. It's . . .'

He made a sudden dash away from her and for a moment Mica found herself filled with rage. Bear would scare the thing away and then she'd never know what it had been.

He came back quite soon, shaking his head.

'I should have picked up my axe as I came out,' he said, regretfully. 'Still, I've frightened it off. There's no need to worry, now.'

'I wasn't worried before,' pointed out Mica.

Bear shook his head, smiling again. Mica could only see his silhouette, but she was certain he was smiling.

'You're really brave, Mica,' he said. 'But you're only a young one and you should take more care.'

Only a young one! As if he'd grown strong and hairy in a single afternoon!

'You know,' he went on, 'I think it must have been a lion. It was big enough, and it moved too quietly for anything else.'

Far away the strange call came again. The quality of the sound was unmistakable, even though it was a quite different noise from before.

'That doesn't sound like a lion,' said Mica, drily. 'That sounds more like someone wetting themselves laughing.'

Bear cocked his head.

'Really? Well, I chased it off, anyway, and that's the main thing. I suppose it must have been a hyena, then. I did only catch a glimpse of it. But you need to be careful going out after dark, Mica. It's dangerous if you don't have fire. I'll always come out with you if you need to leave the shelter.'

There were all sorts of things Mica could have said, but they needed saying quite loudly and that would have disturbed the others. But she *could* have said something about being quite as strong as Bear (which wasn't true, admittedly, but *had been* true until the last season or so) and quite as capable, too.

She got as far as drawing in breath to say something very dignified and possibly just a bit cutting.

But Bear's shape was somehow so familiar and comfortable that she couldn't work out how to do it.

Chapter 7

The morning brought proof that there had really been something in the clearing in the night. The stones over the pit where Amber had hidden away the half-dried strips of meat had been disturbed, and several pieces had been taken.

Seal scowled.

'I heard someone moving in the night,' he said, shooting round suspicious glances from under his heavy brow-ridge. 'Someone went out of the door.'

Elk squatted down and peered at the specks of ash the wind had scattered across the clearing.

'This is strange,' he said. 'Not beast-work or stoneman work. Look!'

There was a footprint in the wind-scattered ash, but it was too long and narrow to be a stoneman's.

'But there's nothing in the valley that leaves such a print,' said Amber, puzzled, peering at it.

Garnet gave it a sour glance.

'If I had caught it—'

Elk laughed, but kindly.

'Even *you* would have trouble getting hold of

nothing,' he said. 'For Amber's right. Nothing makes such a print. This must have been caused by some freak of the wind.'

Mica felt confused.

'Does the wind steal meat?' she asked.

Elk peered into the meat pit.

'Not very much,' he said cheerfully. 'A handful of strips at most.'

'Even a *little* is important, now we have no spears,' snarled Seal, glaring round at the others.

'Well, we must have new spears, then,' said Elk, briskly, rubbing his hands together. 'We'll search along the river—'

'Which is already close to freezing, *Strongest*.'

Seal spoke Elk's title like a challenge; but Elk went on, unperturbed.

'—and perhaps we'll find new spear shafts there. The river's never let us down before, now, has it? Now, where's Pearl? Put out a good piece of the mammoth, old one, and we'll eat.'

'I think I saw the thing that took the meat last night,' Mica told Amber, quietly, when Mica had finished chewing one last mouthful of the still-juicy meat for Pearl.

Amber began to tease out the knots in Mica's hair. Mica's hair was all woolly curls, and it tangled itself up horribly.

'You must have been dreaming, young one,' she said softly. 'No one can see the wind.'

'No, but—'

Pearl champed on her meat.

'That child was born saying *no but*,' she said indistinctly. 'I've been hoping she'd grow more sense as she got older, but there's not much sign of it so far.'

Mica tried to turn to her, but only succeeded in yanking her hair.

'*Ouch!* I just want to *know*, that's all.'

Pearl shrugged her scrawny shoulders. She always ate heartily, but just lately she'd been losing more and more weight until now her face was all bones and hollows. But then Pearl was very old. She'd given birth to Elk when she was three hands of seasons old, and Mica had been born when Elk was the same age. Mica would be three hands old herself in a couple of seasons, so that meant Pearl was old beyond counting.

'But there is nothing *to* know,' muttered Pearl, crossly. 'The wind is nothing. It cannot be seen, so it is nothing.'

'That's right,' said Amber, gently. 'It cannot be seen—or held, either. So it is nothing.'

'But how can it be nothing when—'

But here was Elk bustling up.

'Mica,' he said, 'you have good eyes. Take Lynx for a walk along the river. Look out for wood.'

Amber let go of Mica's hair. Elk was Strongest, and was to be obeyed at once.

'Take care,' she said to Mica. 'Don't trust the ice, it's still thin. And keep an eye out for lions. It should be all right with two of you, but—'

But of course Mica would take care, and of course the ice was not to be trusted, and of course she would keep an eye out for lions. Amber was always telling Mica things she already knew. That was perhaps even more annoying than Amber's refusal to talk about the things Mica *didn't* know.

Mica was still feeling irritated as she walked along beside the river. It was running quietly now that its banks were beginning to ice up, but the sound of the gurgling water still held some echo of the voices she'd heard in the night. How could *nothing* have taken the meat? It was impossible, whatever the others said. How could she have seen *nothing*? How could *nothing* make those noises?

'Lynx!' she called. 'Keep off the ice! It's not safe yet!'

And, most of all, how could the others not be curious? Not-knowing made walls around them, made them half-blind.

But perhaps that made them feel safer.

There was a splash and a momentary flash of brightness.

'Big fish!' shouted Lynx, pointing.

Mica had often wished fish could be eaten, but their blood was cold and gave no strength to a stoneman. It was a great pity.

'Look, Mica, look!'

Lynx had found a piece of wood washed up on the bank. It was stubby and flat and no good for a spear, but it might do as a scoop or a stirrer.

'That's a good find, Lynx.'

'I'll find a spear next!' shouted Lynx, in triumph. 'I'll find a *spear*!'

Mica smiled after him as he ran off. Lynx was right, though, and she must concentrate on searching the streak of shining water which might be hiding anything. You really couldn't blame the others for not dwelling on mysteries, especially now both spears were broken. How could the stonemen kill even a horse without spears, let alone a mammoth or an aurochs or a woolly rhinoceros?

Perhaps—it was hard to believe, but just perhaps— the stonemen's lives in the valley really were coming to an end. Mica had always believed Elk and Amber would look after everything; but how could even Elk find a way out of this?

Mica found her steps faltering. She'd been so busy since the mammoth had died that it was only now she was really properly realizing what was going to happen.

The stonemen couldn't hunt, and so they couldn't build up a store of meat for the winter.

So that meant Pearl was right.

Unless something happened, the stonemen would all be dead by spring.

Chapter 8

Mica was concentrating so hard on the glittering, shifting water that it was a while before she realized that she could hear the calling again that she'd heard in the night. It was low and dipping, as varied as a lark's voice, though with only a little of a lark's energy.

She looked round. There it was again, almost lost in the buffeting wind. It sounded even stranger in the daytime, even more unlike anything that belonged to the valley.

And there, again. Wavering like the river, or like the tale of a hunt. Intriguing. Close.

Irresistible.

Yes, irresistible: there was something in the sound that was pulling at her, promising all sorts of things she didn't understand.

She ran along the river bank until she caught up with Lynx.

'Stay here,' she told him, rapidly. 'Don't go off. Don't go on the ice.'

'What shall I do, then?'

'Just stay here and watch out for wood coming along.'

She turned hurriedly away from the river and started to run up the slope across the wind-rocked grass.

That voice wasn't coming from far away, but it wasn't going to be easy to pin down. One moment it was bouncing off the scabs of ice and snow that littered the hillside, and the next it was shivered by the wind into glittering confusion.

But still . . .

. . . yes. There, over there! There was something over there, moving through the grass. Mica didn't know why, or how, but it was suddenly hugely important that she caught up with this creature and got to understand its calls.

(Yes, that was something she'd not realized before: these calls, so heart-tugging, so echoing, were full of *meaning*.)

Mica hurdled an ancient ant hill and began to sprint. She was slim and long-legged and by far the fastest of the stonemen. She reached the top of the slope and . . .

. . . and then she heard something new: a high sound, ringing through the chilly air.

She knew exactly what that sound was: hyenas.
Hyenas!

And she was suddenly filled with horror. There were hyenas on the hill, and she'd left Lynx alone by the river with no one to guard him.

She turned and threw herself back down the slope,

leaping from one ice-furred tussock to the next, concentrating absolutely on placing her feet so she didn't slip and twist an ankle.

'Lynx!' she shouted. '*Lynx!*'

No answer.

'*Lynx!*'

The wind was behind her. Any answer would be whisked away.

Here. The river bank.

Empty.

No Lynx! No Lynx anywhere.

But no, no, those hyenas couldn't have dragged Lynx away so quickly. They *wouldn't* have done. They'd still be circling him, slipping in to nip and snatch and jump away.

Mica sprinted along the river bank. Lynx *must* be here somewhere.

Nothing. Nothing.

If only she'd ignored the calling of that strange voice. If only she hadn't let it lure her away.

'*Lynx!*'

Nothing.

Could he have fallen into the river? She'd told him to stay away from the—

What was that? Something. Something moving amongst the reeds.

'*Lynx!*'

She almost screamed his name that time; and at that the creature in the reeds stood up and looked round, grinning, and it was Lynx. For a moment Mica

38

wasn't sure whether she wanted to hug him or wallop him; but she was actually too out of breath and weak with relief to do either.

'Look what I've found!' announced Lynx, proudly.

It was a good-sized tangle of wood and riverweed. Lynx had got hold of it, but it was too heavy for him to get out of the water.

'Good,' said Mica, gasping for breath. 'That'll be good kindling, Lynx.'

She helped him pull it out onto the bank. It was an old root by the look of it, and would make a fine fire on a freezing night. It'd be a real pain to lug back to the shelter, but Mica didn't mind that. She didn't mind anything as long as Lynx was safe.

'I hope you're feeling strong,' was all she said. Her own knees were shaking and she felt as weak as a new-born hare.

Lynx puffed out his chest. 'I'm as strong as a LION!' he said, and roared to prove it.

Though not as strong as a pack of hyenas, thought Mica, still breathless.

She got hold of the root and began to drag it backwards towards the clearing.

They met Elk halfway. He was coming to see how they were getting on.

'We found some wood, we found some wood!' shouted Lynx, full of glee.

Elk told him he was a fine hunter, but his cheerfulness rang a little false as his gaze went past Mica to the icy river.

Seal was right. The river was freezing fast, and there was no chance of anything big enough to make a spear being brought down before spring. Unless some miracle happened the stonemen would starve before then.

But Elk was still the Strongest of the Men. He picked up the root with one mighty roar of effort and carried it on his shoulder all the way to the shelter, with Lynx, full of pride and delight, jumping round him all the way.

Mica followed them.

And as she did she wondered if the creature on the hillside had known about the hyenas before it'd started to call to her.

Chapter 9

By the afternoon the skittish wind was chasing away the clouds to reveal a clear pale sky.

'It's going to be a cold night,' said Amber.

Pearl turned her face towards the wind and sniffed loudly. Even Pearl's nose was beginning to look thinner—it'd practically been elk-sized before—but her sense of smell was still very sharp.

'More ice,' she agreed. 'Yes, the river will be solid in another day or so. I can tell from the sound.'

Mica scooped up a handful of mammoth brains. They felt like mashed slugs in her hand. She shuddered and began to rub the stuff into the reindeer skin that was stretched on the ground in front of her. If you didn't do that the hide would soon rot.

Why do brains stop a hide from rotting? Mica had asked, time after time; and each time someone had said *it is the way it happens.*

And they always managed to say it as if that was a proper answer, too.

'It never used to be so cold at this time of year,' said Pearl, rubbing more cold brains into the hide. 'When I

41

was young we had seasons when we hardly let down the door of the shelter.'

'So you have told us,' said Amber, patiently. 'Still, summer will come again.'

'If you can call what we've been having lately *summer*,' said Pearl. 'There's more heat in a heap of day-old wolf-dung than there was in the sun last season. I think the sun's dying down, myself. It stands to reason. It may still be bright, but everything cools down if it's left.'

'Not—'

'—I mean, you don't come back to something and find it *hotter*, do you? In any case, when I was young the old ones were always saying the same as I am now. The years are getting colder and the winters longer. Our Strongest when I was young, Deer, we called him, even spoke of great reeds that grew taller than a man. Trees, that was right, that was their name. *Trees*. Like the birch and juniper we have now, but two or three men high. Spears you could just pluck as you needed one.'

She rubbed her handful of brains thoughtfully between her gnarled fingers and went on:

'I think we're going to end up in an age of ice, myself. That's what's coming, you mark my words. An Ice Age.'

Seal, prowling back to the shelter bearing a last few ragged pieces of meat from the mammoth carcass, snorted as he passed behind them. He didn't think much of Pearl's memories, especially when she started talking about the cold—which was, admittedly, most of the time, just lately.

But whatever was wrong with Pearl's memory there was nothing wrong with her ears, and she'd heard Seal's snort.

'I have lived long!' she shouted after him, baring outraged gums. 'And I have forgotten more than you will ever know, hunter-man!'

Seal hurled the pieces of meat down and rounded on her angrily, his fist raised; but Amber was on her feet and she was between the pair of them at once, smiling and soothing.

'Pearl is old,' she said. 'Most of her life is past, Seal. Her memories are the most precious things she has left.'

Seal glared at her, but Amber put a hand gently on his arm, almost stroking it, until gradually the violence faded from Seal's face.

Mica let out the breath she didn't know she'd been holding and turned thoughtfully back to her work.

Seal had a dangerous temper that led him into all sorts of follies, but he would be Strongest one day, for all that. Elk had a chest like a cave bear, but Seal was a hand's-width taller. It was only Elk's cunning that had kept Seal in check so far.

Seal would challenge Elk sooner or later, and suddenly this challenge seemed very close. Perhaps it was because there was change happening all round them: the spears were broken; Bear was grown-up; and there was a creature in the valley whose calls made Mica shiver with longing.

'I remember one time,' went on Pearl, obstinately. 'There was a full moon. We killed a mammoth and the flesh stayed warm for days. *Days*. Oh, that was a time! I had teeth, then.'

There were footsteps on the path and Garnet and Bear came into view, bright-faced with the cold. Bear was carrying a limp furry body over his shoulder. They'd managed to catch something, then, though it was nothing of any size. It was too dark for a fox, so what . . .

Bear ambled up to Mica and, rather shyly, dropped the corpse in her lap.

'For you,' he said.

Mica recoiled, and shoved the slightly warm thing onto the ground. It landed on the ground with a toadstool-like wobble.

'A glutton!' exclaimed Amber, admiringly. 'Oh, that's fine, Mica. There's nothing so good to wrap round your head as glutton fur.'

And this was true. No one could eat glutton meat, for it was foul with the scent of the thing, but the fur of a glutton never grew frost however much you breathed on it.

Gluttons were horribly hard to catch, though. They were also just about the most nastily vicious beasts that ever set foot in the valley.

Mica turned to Bear to ask him how on earth he'd managed to get hold of a glutton.

But there was something so hopeful about Bear's expression, something so shy and yet certain at the same time, something so *grown-up*, that somehow she couldn't quite bring herself to do it.

'We'll strip the pelt down tomorrow,' went on Amber, happily. 'It'll be wonderful, Mica.'

Yes, it would be wonderful.

Mica made herself smile at Bear.

'It's wonderful,' she said.

And Bear looked as pleased as if she'd given a present to him.

Chapter 10

'We must fit stone points to all the pieces of spear we've got,' said Elk, that evening, when they were eating.

Garnet pushed out her heavy lower lip. She was particularly sullen because the day's hunt hadn't come anywhere near killing anything, even though they'd been out searching the valley for hours.

'How do you think we'll be able to kill a mammoth or a rhino with little bits of spear like that?' she demanded. 'Even a horse could do us a lot of damage if we have to get that close to it. Break our bones like reeds, a horse's hooves could.'

Seal nodded, scowling out through his coarse black hair, but Elk only rubbed his hands together. You could hardly ever dent Elk's determined cheerfulness.

'Our spears will be short, but we'll have a handful of them,' he said. 'We'll work together. Be lightning fast. A stab to the shoulder, a stab to the heart, a stab to the eye and there you are! Warm meat, and full bellies.'

Seal grunted disbelievingly.

'That's easy to say.' He spoke with open scorn and Mica tensed. Was this the moment when Seal would challenge Elk? Reach for his axe?

Elk's bright eyes flickered up at Seal for an instant, but then he yawned and reached down inside his foot-hide to have a good scratch. For a few seconds the only sound in the clearing was Elk's horny nails scratching his flea-bitten ankle.

'Yes, it's easy to say,' he agreed at last, mildly. 'And it'll be easy done, too, if we all work together, you mark my words.'

But Seal gave a snarl and got to his feet. He threw out his great chest, towering over them all.

'Do you say I spoke ill?' he demanded, and put his hand close to the fold in his furs where he kept his axe.

Everyone sat absolutely still.

Elk sniffed and started undoing the bindings of his foot-hides. Mica could hardly believe it. Seal was standing over him, about to draw his axe, and Elk hardly seemed to have noticed.

'I, say you spoke ill?' asked Elk at last, chuckling at the absurdity of the idea. 'Oh no, friend. I don't want to get on the wrong side of you. Why, that'd probably be the last thing I'd ever do!'

Seal was strong, but he was slow-witted, and this unexpected compliment baffled him. He stood, undecided. Mica was sure she'd have been able to hear the pounding of his great heart if her own had not been thudding so wildly through her own veins.

Garnet was getting quietly to her feet and going to stand at Seal's shoulder. Of course Garnet would support Seal whatever he did.

Beyond her, Bear's face was full of doubt and alarm.

So this was it, then. Seal had gone too far to back down.

Any moment now . . .

And then Seal gave a sudden great roar and charged.

Elk moved as quickly as an otter. He threw himself sideways, and Seal, too heavy to swerve, ended up blundering on into the wall of the shelter.

It took a few moments for Seal to disentangle himself, and Mica wasted not a heartbeat of them: Seal might do anything once this blind rage came upon him. She seized Lynx's hand and dragged him out of the clearing to where the endless grass began. Someone called something after her, but she ignored it and plunged into the dusk.

Soon the whispering of the grass surrounded them.

She made for a place where an ancient heap of rhino bones made a mound against the darkening sky and then she pulled Lynx down beside her. They lay, gasping, Lynx's hands gripping tightly onto her furs. After a little while Mica realized he was whimpering.

'He'll come,' Lynx gasped. 'He'll come!'

There was a bellow and then a great crash from the clearing. Mica flinched.

Another crash. It sounded as if Seal was tearing down the shelter. It wouldn't be the first time he'd done that. With any luck he'd exhaust his temper that way, but if not . . .

There were quick footsteps approaching, now, and then a low voice.

'Mica?'

That was Bear.

'We're here.'

'Quick,' said Bear. 'Give me Lynx and we'll go down by the—'

But over her shoulder Mica saw the dimness shift and there was a great bellowing cry:

'*Lynx*!'

Bear snatched Lynx up and they turned and fled headlong. Seal might do anything when he was in this state, but often he turned on Lynx.

Mica ran as fast as she could across the coarse grey grass.

Chapter 11

The valley had been Mica's home all her life, but in the gloom of the evening the place felt strange, alien: the serpentine bog of the valley-bottom, the grey-glittering ice of the river, the looming hills and the wind-ruffled grass seemed suddenly no longer friends.

Not friends.

As she ran she began to hear again the wavering calls of the mysterious creatures that had been haunting her, and this time it felt as if the calls were forming trails of sound through the air, so it was almost as if she were running through the skeleton of some great beast.

(They must be careful to keep away from the carcass of the mammoth, for it would still be attracting scavenging foxes and gluttons. And yes, of course, that must be how Bear had caught the glutton: he must have cornered it inside the great cave of the mammoth's belly.)

Mica stopped for a moment, gasping for breath. It was nearly dark, and the shivering grass made it hard to hear anything. She discovered there was no sign of Bear or Lynx anywhere. They must have veered away from each other in their headlong flight.

She opened her mouth to call them, but then changed her mind. Seal's rages didn't usually last long, but there was no point in drawing attention to herself. Bear and Lynx would be all right as long as they were together.

It was strange to be out on the hillside alone. She had hardly ever been out by herself in the dark, and never so far from the shelter.

There it was again. A wavering call. It was hard to be sure where it was coming from, but if she went along this way . . .

Mica ran carefully across the tough tussocks of grass. She was nimble compared with the other stonemen, but it would be easy to turn an ankle on a frosted ant hill.

It was very dark, now, but her ears would tell her if she strayed too close to the river, and her nose would tell her if she blundered too near to the great twisting bog. It was dark with rot, and the stink of it rose ceaselessly, to be swiped away by the wind.

But there, *there!* Another call, rising over the bumpy ground.

Mica changed direction a little.

There were stars emerging from the greyness of the sky, now, but they cast little light, and around her the valley was fading into a ghostly invisibility.

Only the scraps of snow gleamed like eyes around her.

There, another call. Mica wanted to sprint towards it, but a single slip might be enough to injure her and if she broke a leg she'd be dead before morning. The cold ground would leach the life-heat from her and lull her into an endless sleep. And that would be if she was lucky. If she was *un*lucky a pack of hyenas might come across her before she died.

What am I doing? she asked herself, suddenly, amazed at her own folly. Why on earth was she chasing through the darkness like this, and after something she didn't understand?

Another call. This one sounded different from the others. Perhaps it was just the way it was echoing off the ice down in the valley, but it sounded . . . fierce. Unfeeling.

Mica came panting to a halt. The grass was muttering and whispering all round her, and she suddenly realized that she didn't know where she was.

That was the oddest feeling. She'd lived in this valley all her life and she knew every pace of it as well as she knew her own hands.

But in this darkness . . .

Another call, this time from behind her.

She whipped round, got her feet caught up in an ant hill, and nearly fell over. She stumbled, but found her balance again. The fierce edge to the call was clear, now. It reminded her . . .

. . . she tried to track down the memory . . .

. . . and she shuddered deeply. It reminded her of hunting: of the determination in the hunter's heart to kill. Of the moment when the ownership of a beast's body moved from the animal to the hunter.

There, another call.

And, oh, but now the calls were full of death! They were still intriguing beyond anything Mica had ever imagined, but they were strong, too, as deadly and determined as the ice which was suffocating the winter river.

Oh, but she was a fool, a fool, a fool to have strayed so far. She must get back at once. Back to the shelter where she would be safe.

Except . . . except that she didn't know where she was.

She didn't know where she was.

Mica looked round, hoping to make out the outline of the hills. But the stars were faint in the new darkness, and there was a mist rising from the cold ground which might soon extinguish the stars altogether.

Oh, but there *was* something! Over there. A small steady glow.

Perhaps Amber had lit a rush to show Mica the way home.

Mica would make her way towards it, and even if . . .

. . . Mica stopped, aghast.

Because there was not *one* small glowing light in

the darkness in front of her, but two: two lights, close together, not far away.

Only a few paces away.

Still, and steady and tepid like the autumn sun.

And Mica recognized them for what they were.

They were the eyes of a lion.

Chapter 12

Mica took in a great breath, but the air was full of terror.

Those lights were the eyes of a lion: *a lion*. A lion, close, and watching her. She could hear its breath rasping in its throat.

And it was here. She was all alone, and here in front of her was a lion.

What could she do?

Keep calm, keep calm, keep calm. (This couldn't be happening. Not to her. Everything couldn't be going to end now. Running away so far into the night had been foolish, but not so bad that it could be the end of everything. The end of *her*.)

The light of the lion's eyes went out for a slow instant and for a moment her hopes soared (it's turned away, it's just killed . . .) and then crashed again as they returned.

But there had to be a way out; there just *had* to be.

She mustn't run. That was something she'd been told again and again. A predator will always chase something which runs, and no stoneman can outrun a lion.

55

Mica was going to run, though. She knew it. As soon as those steady eyes moved (she'd watched lions hunt: it would thrust itself forward in a sudden bounding run) she would lose courage and she would turn and run.

It would be quicker to stay where she was and let it pounce on her, let it squeeze her throat until she was unconscious.

(This couldn't be going to happen. This *couldn't* be going to happen!)

If Elk or Seal were here they'd shout at it, charge in thumping their chests and bellowing. See it off.

(Her heart was in her throat, pounding, pounding: she could hardly breathe, let alone bellow.)

All right, but she was going to do it anyway. (But a lion would never be scared of her!) Charge and shout. Challenge the lion. Terrify it.

(So do it, so *do it now!*)

Mica clenched her fists and let out the loudest scream she could. And then she did it again. And again.

There was a grunting roar and with it a foul stench of decay; but the eyes were still there, still focused on her.

But then—

'*Mica!*'

Bear, oh, that was Bear! Mica was hit by such a wave of hope that she was actually knocked backwards a step.

'Here!' she shouted.

'Where?'

'Here! Bear, I'm here! I'm here! There's a lion! I'm *here*!'

And then at once there was a great bellowing and a trampling from the darkness somewhere over to her axe-side.

'Rarrrgh! Rarrrgh! I'm coming! *I'm coming, Mica!* Look out, lion, here comes a stoneman! *Rarrrgh!*'

The lights of the lion's eyes slid away as it swung its heavy head towards the noise. Bear was stamping and banging his chest and making his voice as deep as he could.

'I'll sup your marrow, you mangy beast! Rarrrgh!' Then: '*Mica! Shout again! Where are you?*'

And suddenly Mica had stopped being afraid. She even remembered to throw out her arms to make herself as big and wide as she could.

'Here! Here! *Bear, I'm here!*'

'*Rarrrgh!*'

And then suddenly the lion had swung smoothly round, apparently unconcerned, and it was jogging away down the hill. Mica couldn't really see it, but she could sense the line of its back moving against some faint sheen of starlight on the grass.

'Mica! Mica?'

'I'm here,' she gulped.

Footsteps crashed towards her and then suddenly there he was in his shaggy furs, arms held wide and high, stomping and bellowing and charging along so fast he nearly knocked her flying.

He saw her at the last moment and pulled her round behind him.

'Where is it?' he gasped, raising his arms again.

'Gone,' gulped Mica.

Bear put his hands on his knees and heaved in breath after breath. Bear wasn't built for long runs. None of the stonemen were, except Mica. She stood close to Bear and felt his comforting warmth.

'Well, I found you,' he said at last. 'That's good.'

Oh yes, it was good. Definitely very good. Mica dug her fingers into his furs.

'Where's Lynx?' she asked, at last.

'It's all right, he's with Amber.'

'Seal—has he calmed down?'

'Oh yes. You know Seal. Tame as a baby.'

So now they could go home. Mica listened as well as she could through Bear's panting. She heard a few far-off hooves and then the thin whinny of a horse, but nothing else save the wind.

Yes. Whatever the creature was that had been calling earlier it had stopped, and the long bones of sound had evaporated into the cold air.

So all there was to do now was to go home.

Chapter 13

Bear finished huffing and panting and began pulling at his furs where the bindings had slipped.

'That was a bit close,' he said.

And then he began to laugh. Bear's chest had begun to grow wide over the last season, and his laugh had grown with it. Beside him Mica was a weed, a slip of a curl-haired bulrush.

Bear was laughing at himself, mostly, for being so out of breath; but Mica was still too frightened to join in.

'We'd better get back to the shelter,' she said.

Bear nodded, still a bit out of breath.

'I ran like a wolf with its tail on fire!' he told her. 'I nearly fell over twice. I must have looked like a washed-up eel trying to right myself!'

When he'd been running at full pelt through the darkness to save Mica's life.

Mica began to lead the way back towards the shelter.

'It's along here,' said Bear, helpfully. 'That way'll take you up to the ridge.'

Bear would be right, of course: Mica hadn't a clue which way the shelter was.

Mica turned and began to follow him through the maze of tussocky grass.

Bear strode along, as sure-footed as a mammoth. The moon was rising above the mist, and now Mica found she knew where she was. Bear was taking the path that would take them down to the river.

She kept close to him: Bear's bellowing would have unsettled every beast in the valley, so they'd have to keep a sharp look-out. The hillside would be full of jittery creatures.

Bear did just love to use his new deep voice. Well, that was fair enough (especially when he was faced with a lion). But still . . . it was unsettling. It meant Bear really was becoming a man, and that really did mean he and Mica were growing apart. Or growing together in a new way, perhaps.

Mica thought about Seal the grown man, and she shuddered—which was silly, because Elk was also a grown man, and Bear would surely grow up to be much more like Elk than Seal.

Oh, but it wasn't any sort of a man she was looking for. Not really. She wanted something . . . but that was the problem, she couldn't *say* what she wanted.

She only knew that now the calling that had sounded through the valley had stopped, the whole valley felt stale and flat and dull.

Mica had been so busy thinking she'd let Bear get quite a long way ahead of her. It didn't matter until a cloud slid over the moon and she lost sight of him.

'Mica?'

But here Bear was, coming back to find her. Yes, here was good, kind Bear, who'd been out hunting all day and who must be longing to get back out of the perishing wind. Bear, the almost-grown-up stoneman.

'I'm here,' she said.

'I thought I'd lost you again.'

He took her hand. He was always warmer than she was because her thin body lost heat quickly.

It wasn't easy to walk hand in hand on this rough ground and she was thinking about taking her hand back when there was a thumping of hard hooves just off to her axe-side and she changed her mind.

Bear sniffed the air, listening. Then he grunted.

'What?'

'There are aurochs over there, too, as well as those horses,' he said, quietly. 'We'd better keep on down this way.'

The giant cattle generally caused no trouble unless you got between one of the great bulls and his cows, but Mica had always had a horror of their wide curving horns. There was a malevolence about the beasts which scared her; a calculating desire to wound which she did not pick up from any other creature, not even from the bad-tempered rhinos.

The moon was still hidden, but suddenly the darkness around her seemed to be squirming, populating itself with warm dark violence; with

nerves at full stretch to sense predator or prey. A
little further on she heard claws clipping along on the
frozen ground—but they stopped, or veered away, or
she'd imagined it.

A wolf, probably.

She kept hold of Bear's hand as they walked
through the darkness.

Chapter 14

Without the moon, it was as if the whole valley had been rolled into an endless dark tunnel. There wasn't room for Mica and Bear to walk together once they'd got down to the river, so Mica came along behind again, shivering and continually pulling at her furs. Her bindings had sagged so much that the pelts at her waist kept flapping up to expose her belly to the icy wind.

But at least there wasn't far to go, now. The wide pool where the herons sometimes fished was just round this bend, and soon after that the track led off up towards the shelter.

Oh, but it was so cold. Her sweat was chilling her, now, and it was so *cold*.

Just as they came to the almost-frozen pool the moon slid out from behind a trail of cloud and lit a line of jinking brightness along the narrow line of open water. They'd soon be at the turn-off to the track, and from there . . .

But what was *that*? Over on the other side of the pool. What was *that*?

Bear hadn't seen it. He was striding on.

But what *was* it?

It looked a bit like a giant beaver, although its face was bald and its shaggy coat was a mad mixture of lengths and shades.

But those furs couldn't be natural! They couldn't be. They must be tied on.

But in that case . . .

Mica made a little *tk!* with her tongue, the noise a hunter makes when he needs to attract the attention of one of his band. Bear halted at once and looked back.

Mica pointed.

The creature was squatting in the moonlight on the edge of the ice. Mica could see the thing clearly, but she herself was almost invisible, sliced into confusing streaks of bright and black by the breeze-tugged reeds.

But what she was seeing was impossible. No creature save a stoneman wore the furs of other animals, so this must be a stoneman.

Except that it wasn't. The hair on its head was as woolly as a rhino, for one thing; and even in the bleaching moonlight it was clear that its face was dark, darker even than her own, as dark as bog peat.

Beside her Bear ducked a little to get a better view through the screen of wind-rocked reeds.

The creature was larger than Mica had thought at first glance. It might be as tall as she was (though under its furs it looked even skinnier). Its nose was ridiculously small and flat, and its eyes glittered from under brows which were hardly ridged at all. Why, the thing looked almost like a baby, though you could tell from its body that it was adult, or nearly so.

The reeds swung sharply in an extra-strong buffet of wind and Mica stepped back hastily to avoid being slashed across the face.

The current was always slow round the edges of the pool, and the margins of the water had long been locked up with ice. Yes, it looked solid enough. If she went out through the reeds she'd be able to get a closer look at the thing. It had something in its hand (it had *hands*, just like a stoneman!) and it seemed to be working with some sort of blade.

Was it making an axe?

Mica put a cautious foot down onto the ice. It felt solid, didn't even creak. The reeds proved that the pool was shallow, anyway.

Bear put out a hand to stop her, but she ignored it.

She went forward three paces through the reeds. The creature was intent on what it was doing and it didn't look up. It was hard to be sure, but the thing it was making didn't look like an axe. It didn't even look as if it was made of stone.

But what else could it be made of?

'Mica!'

Bear's whisper just reached her, but she ignored that, too.

Carefully, ever so carefully, keeping a fringe of wind-harried reeds between her and the creature, Mica edged closer.

Chapter 15

The reeds were restless, swaying as if to peer into Mica's eyes, and whispering, whispering, whispering.

Mica went forward cautiously, checking the ice at every step.

The creature still didn't seem to be aware of her. It was an odd thing, that creature, and as Mica got closer it seemed odder still: like a stoneman, but not a stoneman at all.

Perhaps it had been born wrong. Or perhaps it had been injured.

And yet, and yet . . .

Mica went forward two steps more, and it was then that she suddenly discovered it was making a noise, *the* noise, the one that had been haunting her. This sound was much softer, though. It only just carried across the ice to where she was watching. The sound was . . . well, yes, it was a bit like a howl, except that it was . . .

Mica listened, trying to work it out. It *was* a howl, but it was . . . contented. Yes, contented.

A contented howl? But that made no sense.

She took another step. And then another.

Mica could see what it was doing better, now. It was scratching at something with great care and concentration.

But what was it making? You worked stone with sharp blows. This was more like the way you scraped a hide.

And yet it was nothing like that at all.

Mica took one more step forward. The noise the creature was making was dipping and surging, tripping and . . . and . . . and doing something which somehow lifted her heart.

Yes. Although this sound was low, and stranger than anything she had ever heard in the valley, it lifted her heart.

And then, as Mica listened, suddenly it was as if the hills around her were opening, shaking off the harsh shell of the coming winter, and transporting her somewhere . . .

. . . there was sunlight splashing through a place where the reeds grew up almost to the sky. Except that they couldn't be reeds, for they were branched like huge pieces of lichen.

Trees. That was what they must be. Those were not reeds, but trees, tall trees.

Mica gasped in wonder, because for a moment she seemed to be able to feel, even to *smell* the warmth of that place; the peace of it. Oh yes, this was somewhere where there was time to do more than just work and work and work; where life wasn't devoted simply to trying not to die quite yet.

Mica reached out a hand towards the creature squatting on the far shore of the pool. It was still many paces away and there was a narrow strip of sparkling river between them, but she wanted to catch hold of the sounds it was making, to keep hold of them so she could treasure this vision of a place where—

—and then Bear destroyed everything. He leapt out of the darkness, bellowing, as big as he could make himself, waving his axe and thumping his chest.

At once the creature's noise squirted off into a pinched gargle and before Mica could draw breath it had squirmed around like a startled weasel and shot away into the darkness.

In two heartbeats it was gone, gone absolutely, and all that was left by the side of the pool was a wisp of steamy air.

And soon even that was blown to nothingness by the restless breeze.

Chapter 16

'That got rid of it,' said Bear, breathing hard.

Mica was still looking after the creature. Perhaps it hadn't run very far. If she went after it, then—

—if she went after it then it would run away even further and faster. Thanks to Bear.

'Why did you do that?' asked Mica, dazed with loss.

Bear was still getting his breath back. Great clouds of steam surrounded him, glistening in the moonlight.

'It was too close,' he said.

'But it didn't even know we were there!' protested Mica.

Bear settled his axe back carefully inside his furs.

'It shouldn't be in the valley at all,' he said. 'This is stoneman land. It can feed only us.'

Mica's rising anger subsided a little again at that. Bear was right: they couldn't afford to let anyone else hunt here. The valley hardly fed them as it was, and perhaps this winter it would fail to feed them altogether.

She looked across the channel of unfrozen water into the darkness and wondered if the creature was hiding somewhere, listening to them. It had gone crashing off, but she could hear nothing now. Was it squatting in the grass, or had it crept away?

'What on earth was it?' she asked.

Bear ducked his head, flushing, as if she'd asked him something personal.

'A howlman,' he said.

'A *what*?'

Bear held out his hand to her.

'Best come off the ice,' he said. 'It's too new to trust.'

Mica took one last look after the way the creature— the *howlman*—had gone.

And she saw something.

On the bank where the howlman had been sitting something was gleaming in the cold white moonlight. It was tiny, not much longer than her smallest finger. Perhaps it was just a pebble.

Though the thing was an odd shape—not a usual shape for a pebble. She couldn't see it properly from where she was.

She took two rapid steps and then a quick striding jump got her across the water to tumble forward onto the ice on the other side.

'Mica,' groaned Bear. 'Mica, come *back*!'

She crawled forward and snatched up the tiny gleaming thing. It was still faintly warm from the creature's hand.

'*Mica!*'

The ice was creaking under Bear's weight and he

couldn't follow her. 'Mica, come back!' he said again, anxiously.

'Coming!' she called over her shoulder. She tucked the creature's object safely into her furs and made her way lightly back across the ice, over the channel of water, and through the reeds to the bank where Bear was waiting for her.

Bear heaved a sigh of relief.

'You should be careful,' he said earnestly. 'Those howlmen are dangerous.'

Mica thought of the sounds the howlman had made, that had transported her somewhere she had never known before. About the long trails of howling she'd been hearing rippling through the cold valley, sounds that had awoken in her a deep longing for all sorts of things she didn't understand.

'Did you hear it?' she asked. 'It was wonderful.'

Bear hunched his shoulders.

'They're cunning, those howlmen,' he said.

'Really? Cunning? How do you know?'

'I've seen them before. Long ago. Before I came here.'

'But you were only a few seasons old, then.'

'Yes, but I can still remember it,' said Bear.

He turned away and Mica followed him along the path through the hissing, uneasy reeds. He was walking fast, and it took quite a lot of concentration to keep up with him.

'Where did you see them? Did they come to your hunting ground?'

Bear walked on for a long time before he replied.

'There were a lot of them,' said Bear at last. 'They were thin. Weak. A stoneman could crush a howlman neck with a single hand. So we thought they were no danger.'

'And,' prompted Mica, impatiently, when it was clear Bear wasn't going to say any more.

'And they *were* a danger,' said Bear.

He wouldn't say anything after that.

Chapter 17

The clouds soon hid the moon again, so Mica never got a chance to look at the thing the howlman had dropped. When she ran her thumb over its surface it felt scratched, like a butchered bone. It was warm and almost greasy under her fingers.

If only Bear hadn't frightened the howlman off she might have discovered something more about it. What other visions might have appeared in its wavering song?

Here was the track at last.

The clearing was deserted. The shelter had been put back together again, but as it wasn't much more than a few hides that closed off a natural overhang in the hillside that would have been soon done.

The stonemen had gone in out of the cruel wind, and the door skins were weighed down with rocks.

'Bear!' said Bear, quietly, to announce himself, before he began to move them.

'And Mica,' said Mica.

The shelter felt warm with the breath of the Men. Only Elk was still sitting up on his bed.

He cleared his throat.

'You found her, then,' he said.

Mica went and found her bed beside Amber's.

Elk's part of the darkness shifted a little.

'You were foolish to run so far away into the dark, Mica,' he said. He did not speak angrily, but slowly, carefully explaining, as if there could be doubt at all about anything he said. 'The dark is dangerous for a young one,' he went on. 'You know the perils it contains. Hyenas. Wolves.'

'This blessed cold,' put in Pearl, from her bed.

'Yes,' agreed Elk. 'You might have got lost, or fallen and frozen.'

Seal snorted.

'If she'd been working all day as she should have been she wouldn't have had the strength to go running off all over the valley!' he snapped.

And while Mica was still gasping with the unfairness of this Elk said:

'Well, we shall all rest now, and get strength to work tomorrow.'

'Good!' muttered Pearl, from her bed. 'And about time too. Nothing good ever comes out of the dark.'

'But while we were out we saw—' Mica began— but then Bear began coughing and complaining about his mist-dampened furs in a totally un-Bear-like way, and Amber closed her hand warningly over Mica's. Elk was Strongest, and was to be obeyed.

And so Mica went to sleep with the thing the howlman had dropped still hidden warm and secret in her furs.

*** *

Mica woke up as the first shadows of the new day were easing themselves through the gaps in the walls of the shelter. It was deliciously warm under her cover, but she'd got a stone or something in her bed.

For a moment she didn't know what it was, but then with a heart-skip of excitement she realized. She slipped her hand under her cover and brought out the howlman's little pebble. She held it up to the grey light—but what she saw startled her so badly she dropped the thing as if it were glowing hot and it fell down the gap between her grass bed and Amber's, and out of sight.

Mica lay for a few moments with her heart pounding and her mind racing. The thing had felt like a stone in her hand, but it had been alive. It was impossible, but she'd seen it. She'd seen a tiny reindeer kneeling with its nose held up to sniff the air.

Yes, really, a reindeer with curling antlers and its legs tucked under it.

What an idiot she'd been to let it go! It would have escaped by now.

But perhaps she could catch it.

Mica reached down cautiously between her bed and Amber's. She was afraid it might bite her with its tiny teeth, but . . .

There. There it was. It hadn't moved at all.

She drew it out carefully . . . and found herself filled with a new amazement. The thing was only as long as her thumb, but it was certainly a reindeer: except that it *couldn't* be a reindeer because it was also a pebble.

She turned it wonderingly in her fingers.

No, not a pebble. A piece of mammoth ivory.

But . . . but it was a reindeer at the same time.

Mica held it in the light, her brain dizzy. How could this thing be both? It was as if it were dead and alive at the same time: as if the mammoth they'd killed the other day had pulled itself back to its feet after they'd taken out its brains and its liver; as impossible as if one day the rising sun struck cold onto their skins, or the ice began rippling like water on the river, or it began raining and not-raining at the same time.

She held the thing carefully for fear she should crush it, though it felt as hard as stone. It was scored with lines. Yes, she had seen the creature making those lines last night. The creature—the howlman—had been sitting where the ice reflected the moonlight so it could see to work.

And . . . yes! Suddenly, with a gasp of amazement, she understood. These scored lines were what had turned the ivory into a reindeer. She could see it now. The lines followed the curve of its back, and the branches of its antlers. Even the berries of its eyes had been dug out and then rubbed with charcoal to make them dark.

Mica was warm under her pelt, but she began to shiver with awe and amazement. That creature yesterday, the howlman: its face had looked like a child's, but it must have been cleverer than anything she'd ever imagined. To make a dead animal's tooth into something living. Or *almost* living.

But why on earth had the howlman done it? This thing didn't taste of reindeer (did it? No.). It didn't have the hide of a reindeer, either, or its brains or hooves.

And yet this thing must have taken many hours of careful work to make.

So what was it *for*?

But then, before she could wonder any more, Seal gave a great cough and a snort, and the day began. In the space of a few yawns everyone was getting up, ready to start work so that they could live until tomorrow, so they could work some more, and more, and more, until in the end they woke no longer.

Mica slipped the mammoth-tooth reindeer into her furs. It was hers, her secret. The others would never understand it: it was mysterious and wonderful and useless. They would have no value for it at all.

But it was a great treasure, all the same; and she was almost sure that it held the answers to many of her questions.

Chapter 18

'Oh, you'll learn,' said Pearl. And then she added, darkly, 'If you live long enough. Which you probably won't. No, none of us will live long enough for much. We'll all be starved to death by spring, you mark my words, now our spears are broken.'

There was no sun today. The sky was a giant eggshell of grubby white under which the wind blatted and bashed its way through the valley. Pearl was rubbing a mess of brains into the glutton pelt that Bear had brought home.

Mica tugged up her furs yet again. However carefully she tied her bindings she always ended up with a gap over her shoulder. She probably needed a larger pelt.

'Running about in the dark!' snarled Garnet, sourly. Elk had left Garnet at home today even though Garnet hated shelter-work. Mica suspected Elk had done it just to give himself a break. Garnet had been even more ill-tempered than usual lately, and Seal's outburst the evening before had come close to making her look foolish. 'If you chase the wind you end up with the wind inside your head,' Garnet went on. 'And it's a death-bringing wind, too. Elk's too soft on you.'

Mica would have walked away from the pair of them, but she had been told to build a smoking fire. That meant putting together a core of dried dung to get the fire hot, and then throwing on damp reeds to coax out the smoke. Mica often ended her day stinking of burnt reeds—unless, like today, she ended her day stinking of rotting brains, too.

Still, Mica had the little reindeer tucked securely in her furs, and she couldn't help but shiver with joy whenever she remembered it. That howlman was full of wonders. If only she'd had longer to watch it working last night, to listen to its calls. And she would have done if only Bear hadn't frightened it away. But then Bear was always practical. He had no time for ideas, or visions in the dark.

Mica gingerly picked up another boulder of rhino dung. It was frozen on the outside, but you had to be careful because if it was fresh enough your fingers could go right through the frost and end up covered in filth.

'It's so dangerous out in the valley,' said Amber, gently. 'Especially after dark. You're still too young to face down a lion unless you have fire, Mica.'

Mica had known it would be like this. She'd known she'd be in for a whole day of nagging. But it didn't matter. Nothing mattered, because she had the little reindeer, and the excitement of it was making her blood race inside her.

She put down the piece of dung on the hearth and went back for some more.

'We all know that youth is a time for wondering,' Amber went on, when Mica returned.

'Wondering? Wondering fills no bellies!' growled Garnet, and Pearl nodded so vigorously that a dewdrop fell off her nose to mingle with the mess of brains.

'Look at me!' Pearl pointed out, self-righteously. 'I'm so old my poor bones are near poking through my skin, but I'm still working. You don't see *me* sitting around wondering.'

'That sort of thing just hatches worms in the brain,' Garnet agreed, spitefully. 'I knew a stoneman once. He was a good stoneman, but he got thinking, and in the end he couldn't sleep or hunt for fear of the maggots his own brain had hatched.' She let out a bark of scorn. 'We had to kill him in the end.'

Mica went to retrieve another lump of dung. That howlman must have wondered: wondered and wondered, until it'd brought something into being that'd never been seen before. Mica felt quite hollow with the amazement of it. It had made something completely new. Oh, the *hope* of it!

Seal was back at the clearing when she returned. He looked, if anything, even sourer than Garnet, and he was empty-handed. The hunt had failed again, then.

Elk and Bear were not far behind him, their faces glowing with the cold.

Pearl sniffed when she saw them.

'I thought as much,' she said. 'You'll never catch anything without good long spears. Oh yes, we'll all be dead by spring, all right, starved to skeletons.'

'Mica, bring some meat for the hunters,' said Amber, quickly.

Everything would have been all right if Mica's bindings hadn't gone and shifted again as she was carrying a big hunk of bloody meat back to the others. Before she could do anything about it one of her pelts had come loose and the little reindeer had slipped out of the folds. It fell, hit the frozen ground, and bounced away from her.

It ended up barely a foot's length from Garnet's blunt nose. Mica dived forward to snatch it up, but Garnet's hand shot out faster still.

'What is it?' asked Elk, jovially. 'Does the young one keep a pebble next to her heart?'

Garnet peered at it suspiciously. Then she looked again and let out a squawk of shock.

'It's alive!' she screeched, so frozen with horror that she didn't even drop it. She sat there, her eyes bulging as if she'd got a viper on her palm. 'It's cold, cold as death, husband, but it's *alive*!'

Mica went to swipe it back, but Seal's long arm had plucked the little reindeer from Garnet's hand before she could reach it.

'It's mine!' gasped Mica; but Seal was already raising his powerful spear-arm and he was throwing the little reindeer far, far away. It arched through the air, black against the grubby sky, past the edge of the clearing and far into the long, agitated grass.

Mica found she'd let out a wail of loss. She was going to chase after it, but Elk chuckled, and patted her comfortingly on the arm.

'Now, young one,' he said. 'There's no need for passion. Why, we're brother hunters, we stonemen, and so we must be friends. In any case, you wouldn't want to anger Seal all over a pebble! Not with him so strong!' Elk laughed as if that was the best joke he'd ever heard.

Even Bear smiled.

Seal was still staring after the little reindeer. He waited until he'd heard the small thud of the thing hitting the ground and then he dusted off his hands, nodding grimly.

'That's got rid of it,' he said, with satisfaction.

Garnet was white-faced, still holding out her empty palm as if it might be poisoned.

'It was dead and yet alive as well,' she said, shuddering. 'Cold, and yet a living thing!'

Elk shook his head.

'Well, it's a good thing it's gone, in that case,' he said. 'Why, if life and death aren't different things then where does that leave us hunters?'

Pearl snorted disgustedly.

'Mica always *was* one for picking up dirty pebbles and shells and suchlike,' she said. 'Where have you been grubbing about now, young one?'

'Down by the pool,' said Mica, full of sorrow. 'It was made by a howlman.'

Bear suddenly started coughing again, but he was too late. Everyone had heard.

'A *howlman*?' echoed Seal, suspiciously. 'What's that?'

Mica didn't know.

'A thing like a stoneman,' she said.

Elk laughed, but he looked puzzled.

'A thing like a stoneman *is* a stoneman,' he pointed out.

'No,' said Mica. 'It was different. It had hair like a rhino. And a face like a babe's.'

Seal grunted sceptically.

'More thoughts,' he said, with disgust. 'That one's head is always in the clouds. That is no good for a stoneman. A hunter must always see the valley as it is.'

'But I *did* see it as it was!' exclaimed Mica. 'It was making a . . . a howling.'

Seal spoke roughly, turning to Bear.

'Did *you* see it?' he asked.

There was a pause. Bear looked at the ground.

'It was very dark,' he mumbled, at last. 'I couldn't see anything properly.'

For a moment Mica really couldn't believe what he'd just said.

'But of course you saw it!' she said, even more puzzled than angry to start with. 'You scared it off!'

But Bear only shrugged, and didn't raise his eyes.

'A howlman, eh?' said Elk, looking from one to the other of them. 'Well that's a new one. But Mica, my friend, between us we know every reed and blade of grass from one end of this valley to the other, don't we. And if there had been any creature anything like a stoneman here we would have seen it. You must know that.'

Mica was so wounded and bewildered by Bear's betrayal that she was hardly listening.

'You scared it off,' she said to him, again.

'In any case Bear's right, you know,' Elk went on. 'No one can be sure what they see in the dark.'

Pearl nodded.

'That young one needs to be kept busier, Elk. She wouldn't have time to wander about seeing things then.'

'Oh, we shall all be busy,' said Elk. 'I can promise you that. We've a lot of hunting to do before the cold drives the beasts away.'

He began to rub his hands together in the way he did when he was making plans; but Mica couldn't let the matter rest there.

'But . . . but I *did* see something,' she persisted, still not quite believing what was happening. 'It was like a stoneman, but it had dark skin.'

'Mad,' Garnet muttered. 'And this is just the beginning of it, you mark my words. She'll be raving before long.'

That made Amber speak.

'Shadows are always confusing,' she said swiftly. 'And the howling could have been all sorts of things. A wolf. Or the wind.'

'No,' said Mica, though in some dim way she knew it was stupid to argue. 'Those calls . . . the howling . . .

it was . . . it was full of meaning.' That was as near as she could get to explaining how the calls teased her, stimulated her, bewitched her.

Elk didn't stop smiling, though his eyes were watchful.

'Shadows,' he said, with decision. 'Yes. Yes. That was all it was. Forget it, young one.'

Forget it. Sometimes Elk seemed to think his power extended to the sky. None of them was going to forget this in a hurry.

'I'm glad that little stone thing is gone, anyway,' said Amber, with a shudder. 'It made my head swim. It was a reindeer, but it was a pebble. It was so small it had to be on a far hillside, but it was in Garnet's hand at the same time.'

'It's well gone,' said Seal, definitely.

Elk came and put an affectionate hand on Mica's shoulder.

'Good or bad, it was nothing to fill our bellies or keep us from freezing,' he said. 'So it's no loss to us stonemen. Eh, Mica?'

But Mica wouldn't meet his eye. Of course the little reindeer couldn't feed them, or shelter them, or keep them alive.

But it'd been precious, so precious, all the same; and suddenly she felt as if a cliff had come down in front of her and blocked out the hills and the sky.

She walked away as soon as Elk released her. Bear came over to meet her, but she shouldered her way roughly past him.

Bear had lied. Deliberately lied. He'd made her look a fool. Worse than that, he'd made her look mad. He'd betrayed her, and she could no longer trust him.

As soon as she was out of the clearing she began to run. She ran fast down the track to the river, trying to leave behind her hurt and anger.

But however fast she ran her sense of loss stayed with her.

She'd lost the little reindeer, the little precious reindeer.

And the reindeer wasn't the only precious thing that was suddenly gone from her life.

Chapter 19

The rest of Mica's day was filled with chores and confusion. The chores were nothing new: Elk always kept the stonemen busy. When fingers were occupied and limbs were tired then the stonemen were much less likely to challenge their Strongest.

In fact Elk was cunning altogether. He had a highly developed instinct, for instance, for sorting out small problems before they grew into big ones. Elk told Mica to get herself some strips of leather thong to make herself new bindings for her furs.

'They're so ragged you'll be falling over them soon,' he said.

'Yes, we've got some spare thongs cut,' Pearl told her, when Mica went to find some. 'But they've gone as stiff as bones. You and Lynx will have to give them a good chewing.'

So Mica and Lynx settled down to champ their way along a man's-length of thong. This should have been fun, but Mica was still grieving both for the little reindeer and for her friendship with Bear.

With Lynx everything always ended up as a game, though. He caught hold of one end of the thong and began to run round and round Mica until she had to get up too or be strangled. And then he kept *on* running, round and round, until they were both so dizzy they lost their balance and ended up falling over on top of a big heap of bones Garnet had gathered earlier.

Luckily Garnet had gone down to the mammoth carcass in the hope of catching some weasels, so all that happened was that they got shouted at by Pearl.

That piece of thong seemed to be destined to cause trouble, and it was nearly the end of Elk. Mica and Lynx were sitting down, giving the thong a final tug-of-war stretching to make sure it dried supple, when Elk strode back to the clearing carrying such a huge pile of reeds that he looked like a giant walking heron's nest. And before anyone could do anything about it, Elk had walked with complete confidence straight into the stretched thong and had gone *whoomph!* flat on his face.

There was a moment of horrified silence and then Lynx let out a wail of terror.

'Are you all right?' gasped Amber, white-faced, at last.

And of course Elk was perfectly all right. He was Elk, he was Strongest, and it would take more than a tumble to hurt him.

He pushed himself to his hands and knees, panting and swallowing—and then he looked up at Lynx and let out a huge roar which frightened poor Lynx half to death until he realized Elk was laughing. Elk made so much noise he sent the crows cawing into the sky right over on the other side of the valley.

Elk laughed for a long time, and soon Lynx joined him, marching about and falling over again and again to demonstrate what had happened.

The others never really got round to laughing, though. Elk could easily have broken an arm or a leg. And then what would have happened?

Seal would have taken over as Strongest. In some ways nothing would have changed, because Seal was strong, too.

Except that Seal never laughed as Elk did. He got into blind rages. He didn't notice the small problems which threatened to grow into big ones.

Oh, and there was so much that Seal did not understand, Mica thought, as she did up her new bindings. Seal always boasted about having no time for anything he couldn't hold in his hand, but the things you couldn't hold in your hand were sometimes the most important things of all. Things like freedom; hope; tomorrow.

Beauty.

Trust.

Mica slipped away twice to look for the little reindeer, but the grass was endless and the little reindeer almost the colour of the snow, and she'd found nothing.

Curse Seal!

In fact she could almost say *curse them all*. None of them understood. Not even Bear, who had always been her supporter, her friend.

Why had he betrayed her? Why? Was it because now he was grown-up he had to be part of the band, and believe everything they did?

But if you turned away from things just because you didn't understand them, how could you live, change, grow?

Mica couldn't answer that; but she knew she had never felt so lonely in her life.

Chapter 20

That evening the stonemen sat around the fire Mica had made. The fire gave out more smoke than heat, of course, but there was warmth enough in it to take the teeth out of the wind.

When the pelts were well smoked and the fire had died down the stonemen went into the shelter and weighed down the door hides for the night. Mica was glad to pull her cover over her, for she was exhausted with work and strong feelings.

She fell asleep on her grass bed with the bubbling snores of the stonemen rising around her.

And then it seemed to her that she was standing in the middle of the clearing. She couldn't imagine what on earth she was doing there, for it was nearly dark. In fact the whole place was quiet, so still, that when something gave her a great jolt she nearly fell over.

And that was even odder, because there turned out to be an elk on the ground right there beside her. It had its antlers caught up in a whole mass of thongs that were writhing and whipping and wrapping themselves round and round, clutching at her legs. So Mica kicked out all in a panic to try to get herself free . . .

. . . and found herself falling down the gap between her grass bed and Amber's.

Mica gasped and winced and opened her eyes.

Just a dream.

Just a dream.

She lay there, panting, her heart hammering as if she'd been hunting.

It was all right, it was just a dream.

Pearl said that dreams were just the night mists getting in through your ears so you couldn't see your memories properly. Seal scoffed at the idea, but Mica had always thought it felt true. This elk dream had certainly been a mixed-up memory: it hadn't been *an* elk, but Elk himself who'd got caught up in a thong and fallen on the ground.

Mica eased herself back onto her bed. Seal was snoring like a bull, curse him. How was she going to get back to sleep now?

Yes, curse Seal, all right, for he was the one who'd thrown away her little reindeer. Oh, and the reindeer had been such a treasure. It had come *out of the howlman's mind.*

If only she could work out how to make something new like that herself. Then she could make her own world. Then she could do anything.

But it was no good, because all that came out of her mind were dreams, and what good were dreams?

Dreams were less than air. You couldn't make anything from a dream, whatever it was about.

Unless . . .

And then Mica held her breath because suddenly her dream and the real world were melting together in her mind, just as the whole valley could be melted into a single drop of spring dew.

And she found herself seeing something new. Something completely new.

It was so amazing that she sat up, blinking into the damp chill of the shelter.

And still she hardly dared to breathe in case she disturbed this wonderful, exciting, terrifying idea which was floating and growing and rippling in the darkness round her like a stream of sound.

This was really *something new*: something that had not existed a moment ago. And now it did.

How? How could something have come out of nowhere like that and into her mind?

It was something vitally important, too. Something which might stop them all from starving in the midwinter darkness.

Because Mica had suddenly realized that any elk, not just their own Strongest, might be tripped up with a length of thong.

Chapter 21

'But you can't expect us to waste time on one of your fancies,' said Amber, kindly but a little wearily. 'We're all busy.'

Mica stayed very patient. If anyone was going to listen to her it would be Amber (because she wasn't ever going to speak to Bear). And so Amber had to be made to listen.

'But—'

'The stonemen are fine hunters already,' said Amber, still kindly, but as if that was the end of the whole matter.

'But now we have no long spears—'

'Oh, spears have broken before, Mica, and no doubt will again. But the stonemen carry on. They always will.'

Mica could feel the frustration bubbling up inside her, ready to explode.

'But the winters are colder, now,' she pointed out. 'Pearl says so. And she says there's less game passing through the valley.'

Amber smiled.

'Pearl is old,' she explained. 'She's looking back over a great distance, and things in the distance are hazy.'

'But—'

'*But*, Mica, our ways have kept us alive since the hills rose. Do you really think that something that's just sprouted in your head is more cunning than the ways of all those generations of stonemen?'

It was true that it didn't sound likely, but Mica carried on anyway.

'But if things are changing—'

'Are they? Do we ever wake up and find that the hills have walked into new places? Or that the river has begun to flow the other way, up the valley?'

'No, but—'

'No, of course we don't. Because the hills and the river are heavy, and even the stonemen all together cannot move them.'

Mica opened her mouth to say *but* again, but Amber hadn't finished.

'No more, young one,' she said, firmly. 'I know how sweet new paths look to the young, and I know you don't mean to harm Elk. But if you talk like this it *will* hurt him.'

Mica had thought she was ready to counter any argument, but that really shocked her.

'Of course I don't want to harm Elk!' she exclaimed.

'Then you must think before you speak,' said Amber. 'You know the Strongest is always at risk. Every complaint is a challenge he has to fight off.'

Mica could say nothing to that, because Amber was right. If she unsettled the stonemen then Seal would seize the chance to make another challenge. And Elk wouldn't be able to turn Seal's challenges aside for ever.

Amber was getting to her feet.

'Now, we have skins that need scraping, Mica, or they will be sprouting maggots. Come along, to work! To work!'

Of course, to work: it was always *to work*.

So Mica went to work.

But not *just* to work. Mica might have lost the little reindeer, but it had set her mind whirring in an entirely new way.

The stonemen were facing starvation. They hadn't caught anything at all to eat since they'd lost their spears. They were going to need a new way of hunting if they were going to survive the winter.

Mica never stopped thinking all the rest of the day.

Chapter 22

Mica cornered Bear that evening when he was on his way back from the latrine. He looked so alarmed at the sight of her that she nearly hit him over the head with a rock.

'Why did you tell the others we didn't see that howlman?' she asked, fiercely.

He hunched his shoulders as if in hope of making himself a smaller target.

'Howlmen are dangerous,' he said.

'Weedy things like that?' she asked, with scorn.

Bear bit his lip.

'The stonemen where I was before didn't think they were dangerous, either,' he said. 'But I'm the only one . . . I'm the only one they didn't kill.'

'*What?*'

'I was small,' he said, unhappily. 'I never understood most of it. They all went off to hunt the howlmen, I think. I know they were in such a hurry that they left a great bear fresh-killed on the hillside. So I waited and waited. But it wasn't the stonemen who came back. It was the howlmen. I heard them calling as they came up the track, and so I ran away. And when I went back there was no one at the shelter any more. And the place smelt of blood.'

'But why did you pretend we didn't see the howlman?' Mica demanded. 'If they're that dangerous—'

'Because if Seal knew about that howlman he'd want to fight it, wouldn't he,' he said. 'And then Elk would have to lead a hunt. And then the howlmen would kill us all, just like they killed my mother and father and everyone. I was just trying to keep us all alive, Mica.'

Oh, but it was hard to be angry with Bear.

'Well, I'm trying to keep us alive, too,' said Mica. 'And I've had an idea.'

Bear did listen. But at the end he said nothing.

'So?' said Mica. 'What do you think?'

Bear ducked his dead-grass head.

'All that . . . it's just come out of your head,' he said, awkwardly.

It's just come out of your head. Mica nearly *did* hit him over his great fat skull with a rock, then. As if it were impossible ever to change, to move, to grow, to *hope*.

'But it could still work,' she said fiercely.

Bear flinched away from her anger.

'Couldn't it?' Mica demanded.

Bear flicked a pleading glance at her.

'But our old ways have always worked all right,' he said, pathetically. 'There's no need to change.'

Honestly, it was like trying to reason with a cliff.

'But this is something *extra*, Bear! It won't stop us carrying on the old ways too.'

Bear kicked miserably at the ground. At last he said:

'That elk you saw . . . that was only a dream, Mica. Dream food doesn't make a stoneman strong. I wish it did, but it doesn't.'

'No,' agreed Mica, desperate for him to understand. 'But a dream might . . . it might shine a light on things that are real, all the same.'

Bear still wouldn't look at her. He was so large and shambling, and yet at the same time as meek as a fawn. Oh, but it really was hard to be angry with him.

She moved close enough to whisper.

'We could make it a secret,' she suggested. 'We could go out early in the morning before anyone else is awake. Take out a piece of thong and see if we can use it to trip up a beast. That can do no harm, can it? Because only you and I will know.'

But Bear only twisted his hands together.

'You should forget this, Mica,' he said, miserably uneasy. 'This thing's—it's come from nothing, so it can't be anything. Please, let it go.'

He went as if to walk past her back to the clearing, but she didn't make way for him.

'Do you *want* to starve?' she asked. 'Do you want us to die in the midwinter dark?'

He didn't answer and suddenly she wanted to shake him.

'You know we're not going to survive this winter, don't you,' she said.

'We might,' he said helplessly. 'Another mammoth might come along and die, like the one that died over on the other side of the valley when we were small.'

'Oh yes, that's likely, isn't it,' said Mica, with scorn.

He winced, but then he took a deep breath and clenched his fists as if trying to summon up his courage.

'Mica,' he said. 'If you keep setting out on new paths like this you'll get lost.'

'Discovering somewhere new isn't the same as getting lost!'

'Lost in your mind,' Bear said. Then he looked at her properly, seriously. 'Mica, if . . . if you chase something that's not real then your thoughts will thicken into a fog. You won't be able to see what's real any more. And then one day you won't be able to find your way back.'

Mica snorted.

'There's not much point in finding my way back if there's nothing to eat when I get there,' she snapped.

Bear hesitated at that. And then he took another deep breath and said:

'Look, Mica, things are difficult at the moment. I'm going to have to work really hard if we're to survive. I have to be grown-up. So I'm sorry. I'm really sorry. But there's no time for me to play any more.'

And then he moved her gently out of his way and went quietly back to the clearing.

Mica was left staring after him. The fool, the idiot, the *stoneman*! This idea of hers might save them all, and he wouldn't even think about it.

None of them would.

And winter was on its way.

Oh, but she was alone, so alone.

So *alone*.

Chapter 23

The wind grew stronger as the evening went on. Everything that wasn't weighed down kept being whisked away, or tumbled along the frozen ground, or wrapped round people's faces. Lynx spent the evening joyfully chasing things, and Mica kept grabbing at things, feeling her bindings come loose, and cursing.

'You've grown, that's the trouble,' said Amber, helping Mica re-bind her gaping furs for the third time. 'New bindings aren't enough. We need to find you some bigger pelts.'

Amber was right, though the problem was partly that Mica was a different shape from the others. The other stonemen were sturdy and round-chested, and compared with them Mica was built like a starved reed. Mica only had to reach for something for a gap to open up between her pelts and for the frozen air to dive down to goose-pimple her skin.

Once that evening she actually managed to lose a pelt altogether. She felt her bindings shift, and before she could do anything about it the whole skin was flapping crazily round her head. The next thing she knew it was flying away like a tattered heron and off out of sight into the grass.

Mica let out a scream of rage and charged after it and Lynx chased after her, whooping like a hunter.

It hadn't gone far, of course. Mica threw herself on top of it and then sat and wrapped it back round her as securely as she could. The sound of Pearl's snickering laughter from the clearing did nothing to improve her mood.

Lynx's gleeful face appeared through a tuft of grass.

'You ran as if there was a lion after you!' he said.

Mica thought about clumping him one; but then she managed to grin, too.

'Another minute and I'd have turned into a stoneman-shaped icicle,' she said, tucking her furs round her as securely as she could.

She looked round in the grass for the little reindeer as she got up, but it was hopeless. The thing was tiny and the grass went on for ever.

She made her way back to the clearing. Pearl was nagging her before she'd even sat down.

'Running about when you should be working!' Pearl snapped. 'You'd better come and shelter this fire for me if you've got nothing to do!'

It was another smoking fire. The rolled hides were suspended in what should have been the thickest part of the smoke, except that the fluky wind kept swiping the smoke away into wisps and fragments. Mica stood with a hide held behind her to make a windbreak, and the smoke at once grew calmer. It began to rise in curls and swirls until it started to make her feel quite dizzy.

It was odd, she thought dreamily, but the curls of the smoke reminded her of something. They were a little like Lynx's hair, of course, but it wasn't that. It was something else which moved and twisted and turned . . .

And then she realized. Yes. It didn't really make much sense, but the swirling of the smoke reminded her of the calls of the howlmen. The smoke moved through the air in the same sort of way, except that it was made of dust instead of . . . well, breath, perhaps, or pulsing ideas.

But that was so strange, so astonishing, that Mica didn't even hear when Pearl told her she could take the windbreak down.

How could there be any link between this smoke and the sound of the howlmen's calls? It made no sense at all.

Did it?

Chapter 24

The howlmen's calls sounded all round the shelter that night. They called and called until Mica was forced to sit up out of sheer restlessness. Their voices, now harsh, now thin, rippled through the cold air, transparent as mist, but hard with power.

And now she found she could see something new in the sounds, too. Instead of formless trails of smoke she could make out shapes. They were constantly changing, but the calls made arches, spears, spirals . . .

She listened and listened, hoping suddenly to step into some real understanding of the patterns. She even got up and slipped out to stand with her back to the shivering hide door.

The air was so cold it hurt to breathe, and the furred edges of the door hides were frozen and prickly under her hands. Above her in the black sky the stars were clustered thickly, shining like tears in the infinite darkness. And as she stood there the drops of light somehow merged with the howlmen's calls into a web of . . . she didn't know what it was, but it was something precious and thrilling and overwhelmingly important.

She gazed for a long time into the call-trailed darkness beyond the clearing, but she saw nothing. So she looked up at the stars again—and was suddenly giddy.

They'd moved. The stars had moved. She was sure of it. The whole sky had swept itself round in the time she had been standing there.

Do the hills move? Amber had asked her only that morning. But perhaps they did, for the sky had moved, and that was even vaster than the hills.

The sky was moving, moving, like the calls of the howlmen and the smoke of the fire and the summer river.

And suddenly Mica's head was crowded with images: a herd of reindeer trotting along the valley; the grass bending and bouncing away from the wind; the movement of her own feet as she walked along an ancient track.

Everything, she realized, *everything* was moving. There was no stability. Everything was part of this constant ceaseless movement.

The stonemen said the world would never change; but if even the sky moved . . .

Mica still didn't completely understand what this meant, but she could feel the excitement of it thumping and surging inside her.

Chapter 25

Mica was still fizzing with excitement when she woke up. Every single thing in the whole valley had suddenly become utterly fascinating: the grasses that bowed their heads in the wind, the smudge-edged clouds, even the frozen grain of the mammoth meat she ate for her breakfast.

'That boy's scratching is spoiling my meat,' growled Seal, glaring across at Lynx.

'Lynx!' snapped Garnet. 'Can't you sit still?'

Pearl put out a skinny arm and pulled Lynx towards her to sniff at his head with her sharp nose.

'He'll have got lice again, most likely,' she said.

Elk nodded, and his great shoulders, which had tensed up a little, relaxed.

'Well, that's soon sorted out,' he said. 'Mica, clean Lynx's hair this morning.' Mica's eyes were the best at close work. 'And you'd better help him shake out his bed furs, too.'

Lynx's hair was coarse and curled and dark, and the pale lice eggs showed up well. Mica scraped the nits away with her nails and picked out any lice she could find, while all the time Lynx fidgeted and sighed and complained that his hair was getting pulled.

'Well, sit still, then!' said Mica. 'Now, let me look behind your ears. Ah. Loads, here.'

'I don't mind having lice,' said Lynx, without much hope.

'No. But Seal minds,' said Mica, darkly.

And at that Lynx gave a huge injured sigh and stopped arguing.

The back of Lynx's hair had got matted together with fur from his clothes. There was no avoiding pulling those bits however careful Mica was.

'There,' said Mica, at last. 'That'll have to do for now.'

Lynx got up fast in case she changed her mind and then he put up his hands to his head and scratched and scratched and scratched, putting tangles back in where Mica had just laboriously straightened them.

'Why you little . . . '

Lynx squawked and fled and Mica had chased him halfway down to the river before she realized what she was doing.

She pulled herself to a stop.

'Hey, Lynx!' she called. 'Come back! It's all right, I'm not really angry!'

She gazed out over the sea of uneasy grass. She couldn't see Lynx. He could be hiding anywhere.

'Lynx!' she called, again.

No answer.

Mica jogged on down the track. He couldn't *really*

think she was going to hurt him. After all, she never had before.

'Hey, stop messing about!' she said. 'If we're caught out here when we should be working we'll both be in trouble!'

That did it. She saw something dark bob up from behind a tuft of grass and Lynx appeared, grinning at her.

'You're not going to pull any more of my hair out, are you?'

'Not unless you keep on annoying people with your scratching,' said Mica, greatly relieved. The grass looked empty, but it could be hiding a whole pack of hyenas for all she knew. 'Anyway, it's not my fault your hair was all tangles. You should keep it groomed.'

Lynx's untidiness was Garnet's fault if it was anyone's. Lynx was hers, but she was too busy hunting to care for him much. That was left to the others.

Lynx came back to Mica, quite cheerful again.

'I bet mammoths have terrible tangles,' he said. 'I bet mammoths have tangles lots worse than I do. I bet a mammoth's tangles are *this big*,' he finished up, holding his arms wide.

They began to walk back along the track.

'I bet you wouldn't like to be a mammoth, would you, Mica? It'd take you all day to get rid of all the knots in your hair.'

'It'd be terrible,' Mica agreed. 'Especially if I had to try to undo them all with my nose.'

Lynx let out a shriek of delight and began banging his nose into Mica's furs and making mammoth-noises.

Mica laughed, but then stopped because suddenly the excitement of last night had come back to her. Some memory of the constantly moving world. It was something to do with the mammoth. With tangles. With hair and fur matted together. Yes, there was some echo of something there, some connection, but she couldn't quite reach it.

She grabbed Lynx's hand.

'Come on,' she said. 'We'll go back the river way and have a look at the mammoth. I'll race you. It'll warm us up after sitting still so long.'

Lynx gave a whoop of excitement and started running, and Mica ran along after him. She felt as if she were on the verge of discovering something: of joining things together in some quite new way to reveal . . .

'Beat you!' shrieked Lynx, at last, in triumph.

The great beast was almost submerged, now. It was only the ice that had formed round it that was holding it up. One huge tusk curved up through the air, out and round and then down again to pierce the ice.

'It's all eaten up,' announced Lynx, with satisfaction.

Lynx was right. All that was left was the bones, and some fragments of skin.

Mica drew her axe and, stepping gingerly over the ice, cut off a good handful of the long hair.

'What do you want that for, Mica?'

The mammoth's skin was tattered into holes at the edges where it had been chewed by small creatures—weasels, most likely.

Tattered into holes . . . oh yes. *Yes!*

Mica felt a glow of triumph spreading through her despite the bitter wind. This was it, the way it all fitted together to make something new. Something completely new. Yes. *Yes.*

'Come on,' she said. 'We must get back to work or we'll be in trouble. I bet you can't beat me on the way back.'

Lynx raced off and Mica ran along behind him, possibilities falling into place around her as she went.

'What are you *doing?*' asked Amber, in horror.

Mica jumped. She was wrapped in her bed fur and had all the various bits of her wearing pelts scattered round her.

Amber peered at what Mica was doing.

'Why are you making holes in your furs?' she asked, utterly shocked.

'To make them warmer.'

'But—'

'Look,' said Mica, swiftly. 'See? I have used this mammoth hair to tie the furs together. Now it won't gape any more however much I run or move about.'

Amber looked, and blinked, and looked again.

'You've put the hair through the little holes,' said Amber, confused. 'And then you've tied it.'

'And once I've tied all these bits of fur together then there will be no draughty gaps,' said Mica. 'It's an idea I've had. Something new that's come out of my mind.'

Amber hesitated, blinking and uneasy and still a little puzzled. And then she shook her head.

'That's not how the stonemen dress themselves,' she said.

But she was running a thoughtful finger under her bindings as she turned away.

The stonemen were taken aback by Mica's new furs.

Elk walked round her, scratching his head, and Seal scowled at her from the edge of the clearing.

'How could you throw a spear when your fur's all stuck together like that?' he demanded.

Mica shrugged. She'd never had a spear to throw. They were always taken by the immensely powerful men.

Even Bear kept a little way away from her. He was frowning and uneasy.

'What do you think?' asked Mica, challengingly.

'It looks hot,' he said.

'Yes,' said Mica. 'It is. Good, isn't it.'

Elk was still scratching his head.

'It may be hot, but it'd trap the sweat of a hunter,' he said. 'And if it came to a fight . . .'

Seal nodded.

'Stonemen do not tie their furs in this way,' he announced. 'Our fathers and their fathers have lived with their furs bound, and all has been well. This will attract lice and stinks and sickness. And it gives a stoneman a hide like a beast.'

Garnet laughed scornfully.

'No one will ever think *I* am a beast,' she said. 'I am a stoneman, and we are greater than any beast.'

And at that Seal thumped his chest and roared his defiance across the valley.

Chapter 26

The stonemen were already stirring when Mica opened her eyes the next morning. Mica, amazingly warm and comfortable, stayed where she was. Usually by morning her furs had got rucked up and the chilly air was spreading itself through all the gaps between her pelts. But today . . .

'Time to rise, time to rise!' Elk was saying, as brisk as ever; and Mica regretfully pushed aside her cover and got up.

Pearl was moving cautiously: lately she'd been waking up with her joints so stiff they were almost solid. She seemed to be getting thinner with every passing day.

Elk drew aside the shelter door to reveal an icy world where every blade of grass was sting-edged with frost.

Mica ducked out through the doorway and stood drawing in deep breaths of the cold air. It was so early the white churned sky was still tinged with the warm feathers of dawn.

This was the first time for moons she'd really *seen*

the dawn, she realized. Usually she was so cold she had no time for anything but scuttling her chilly way towards breakfast without a thought for the sky, or the patterns of the frost.

She sat down to gnaw at the piece of mammoth Pearl gave her. It was frozen on the outside, but inside it still yielded a little under her teeth.

Since yesterday, since she'd succeeded in making something new, everything around her was utterly transformed, filled with possibilities. Suddenly she was sure that everything in the familiar clearing was most marvellously connected with everything else. The scrappy scoops of snow were like the flecking on the shoulders of a great white owl; the frosty grass was toothed like lizards; the icy puddles along the track were like rafts of moons.

Even the tiny tendrils of the bright lichen on the little birch shrubs echoed the mighty spread of antlers.

Mica could hardly breathe with the excitement of being in the middle of all this. Of all these connections, all these patterns, all this possibility. She found herself pushing her finger round on the frost-powdered ground in jerky swirls, and even this was like the path of a moth round a fire.

'What are you messing about at?' demanded Pearl, querulously. 'Stop your fidgeting, will you, you'll give me indigestion.'

Mica quickly brushed the lines away, but the patterns were still in her mind, and the excitement still quivered inside her.

Mica could think of nothing, see nothing, but echoes and connections all day. She was so dizzy with the excitement of them that she nearly scraped a hole right through the hide she was working on.

It was like living in a different world. Even the clearing, which she'd known all her life, had become a completely new place. There were crumbly edges to the dry-frozen earth; a shell-like sheen to her nails; tiny points to each individual filament of fur which showed at her wrists.

Suddenly every single object in the whole place had begun to hum with secret promise.

Bear came back from the hunt that afternoon bearing an armful of bones. The stonemen had failed to kill again, but these bones could be burned. The only trouble was that they took so much heat to set them alight that it was hardly worth doing.

'I think that hide's finished,' he observed, quietly, squatting down beside her. Mica started, and looked at what she was doing, and saw that he was right.

'I was thinking about hunting,' she told him, still fizzing with irrepressible excitement. 'About ways to trip up a deer. Suppose—'

But Bear was shaking his head before she'd even begun to explain.

'A deer goes on four feet,' he said, 'and three is enough. A man could not trip a deer.'

He spoke so definitely that he almost convinced

her, but she went on anyway, buoyed up with the delight of all her new discoveries.

'But we can still try things, Bear. It'll be fun even if it doesn't work.'

He'd been out hunting all day and that was probably why he looked tired to death.

'No,' he said. 'We can't. Seal would go mad, and he's restless enough as it is.'

'So who cares what Seal thinks? He's not Strongest!'

Bear gave her a strange look.

'Isn't he?' he asked. 'How do you know?'

And at that Mica's headlong joy faltered. None of the stonemen knew for certain who was strongest. Bear was right: the last thing they wanted was to get Seal into such a rage he challenged Elk.

'Well, I'll try some new ways of hunting all by myself, then,' Mica said, still trying to keep hold of all this bright discovery.

Bear sighed.

'No one can hunt alone, Mica.'

And at that Mica's brightness finally faded. Faded completely. Even the sky felt suddenly heavy over her head.

Perhaps Bear was right. Perhaps he was. How *could* anyone stampede a beast towards any kind of a trap and be ready to jump on it at the same time?

Bear took the bones to the bone pile and then came back to her again.

'Let it go, Mica,' he said earnestly. 'All this isn't real and it'll do no good.'

'But why shouldn't I think what I like in my own head?' demanded Mica, as fiercely as if she had no doubts about anything at all.

Bear took in a deep breath.

'Because we depend on knowing the valley,' he said. 'Which way the beasts travel, the position of every mound and hollow. We need all that knowledge in our heads because if we lose it we'll starve. Chasing the wind won't feed us, Mica.'

But Bear was wrong, wrong, wrong. He must be, because the valley and even the sky were moving, were changing, and somewhere there was bound to be some idea, some connection, that would help them all.

Oh, but what if there was? The others would stamp it flat, and that meant Mica was as trapped as that gnat in the spider's web that was hung across the doorway of the shelter.

Bear was still speaking, but Mica was no longer listening to him. She was watching that little struggling gnat. And look, there was a shining-haired spider dropping into view to swing in front of its ice-furred web.

And Mica felt the jolt of a collision: of a connection between two things that had never been connected before.

She and Lynx had swung round and round on the ends of that piece of thong until they'd spun dizzily away across the clearing to crash onto the bone-pile.

Yes. *Yes!*

Here, burning itself into her mind, was a way she could bring down a running beast alone.

Alone. She could hunt alone.

Bear was still speaking to her, but it was as if he were miles and miles away.

And she was suddenly hot with excitement even though she was also shivering, as if with bitter cold.

Chapter 27

The image of Mica and Lynx whirling round and round on either end of that thong stayed with Mica all through the rest of the day. Her fingers kept making lines in the ground, and . . .

'Keep your mind on what you're doing, can't you!' snapped Pearl. 'You're no more use than a skinned fox!'

So Mica tried. But that spider, and that thong . . . it wasn't just her new idea that was distracting her, but the extraordinary thought that a spider's web could spark the solution to a completely different problem. She found herself actually shaking with excitement as she thought about it, which was all the time.

'Can I go for a walk?' asked Mica, at last, restless beyond bearing. 'I could go down to the river and look for driftwood.'

Pearl sniffed. 'You might as well, for all the use you're being,' she said. But Amber shooed her away kindly.

'But don't go far,' she said. 'And keep a look-out for beasts.'

'I'm big enough to see off any beast,' said Mica, for the million patterns in the valley made her feel she could triumph over anything.

'All right, then. But come back with your head straightened out, do.'

Mica went off quickly, before anyone could come along and stop her. She ran down the track towards the river, as she'd done practically every day of her life, and every step of the way seemed strange and rich and jangling with echoes and patterns and possibilities. Everything—the curds of the clouds and the hustling of the wind—seemed to be clamouring at her. *Look at me, look at me, here is the secret to everything.*

The river was almost silent, now, a thin pale rippling between the encroaching ice, and all around her were the arches of the hills that held up the cloudy sky. The hills had always been the limit of Mica's world, but of course she'd long known the world carried on beyond them. Bear had come from somewhere beyond the hills, and so had Seal.

(*Seal.* What sort of an animal was a *seal*? She'd often wondered but never dared to ask. She imagined something like a cave bear, but even more bad-tempered and vicious.)

Mica steadied her breathing. There were so many thoughts colliding in her head that most of them were falling over before they got anywhere. Perhaps her mind just wasn't big enough to hold them. She wasn't stupid, but she was certainly odd. Different from the other Men.

Well, she'd always known that. She was skinny, and her legs were long, and her skin was always summer-dark. And yet she'd been born from Amber: so what could she be but a stoneman?

Bear didn't seem to mind her looks, but then Bear . . . oh, Bear was kind. He even loved her, and always had. But there was so much he didn't understand. He didn't understand that she was grown-up now, too, though she'd not grown up into an adult stoneman but into something beyond his imagination. It might turn out that Bear was right, and that no one could live if they let their minds chase all the links and patterns of the world. But still . . .

. . . but still, she couldn't close her mind to all these echoes, these trails of possibility. The spider had made her think of a new way to hunt without spears, and that might make the difference between her living and her starving in the midwinter dark. To think that something so small had led to something that might be so important.

Yes, and this had all started with something even smaller: with the strange wavering calls of the howlmen that made patterns through the air. Patterns that she could now trace, if not understand.

Mica ran along by the river even though there was no longer enough water to bring down any more wood until the spring. That was the best time for the stonemen to find driftwood, when the floodwaters rushed through the valley with the tumultuous thaw.

Not that the stonemen were going to live to see the spring unless they changed the way they hunted. And what was the chance of that?

Alone. Perhaps she *could* live alone, even though the very sound of the word was terrifying.

Oh, but why wouldn't the stonemen *listen*?

Mica turned back towards the shelter. She hadn't gone far when she saw a flower in the snow. A flower, in winter. It was warm and bright, with delicate spreading petals.

And there was another one. And another. A whole trail of them, each one a little bigger than the one before.

And there, over there, was a great churning up of the scanty snow, and stonemen's footprints mixed with the great trampling hoofprints of a mighty aurochs bull.

And over there more brightness, blooming horribly in the snow.

Mica began to sprint.

Chapter 28

Mica chased along the trail of brightness. It led to the clearing. Everyone was clustered anxiously round someone who was lying on the ground.

Someone big, fox-haired. Elk! *Oh no, not Elk!*

Seal was coming out of the shelter with a strip of hide.

'Quick!' Pearl called, screeching, panicking. '*Quick!*'

Elk. It had to be Elk there on the ground. Elk. Injured.

Mica went forward quickly, peering over Garnet's shoulder, wanting to see and not wanting to at the same time.

Elk's face was pale as driftwood; his flesh was oddly greasy, too, shrunken with the strange gleaming look of death.

But he was not dead, for he was moving his head from side to side, again and again, like a dying deer.

Seal was slashing through Elk's bindings, peeling away his dark and sticky furs.

The wound was a ragged tear. It was pulsing bright blood.

'It caught him with its horn,' said Garnet, loudly, almost as if she were arguing with someone. 'It was a great bull aurochs. I tried to distract it, but we only had short spears. It gored him. Tossed him aside as if he were a bundle of reeds.'

Seal laid the patch of hide against the wound and pressed hard. Elk jerked and twisted, and in only a few moments there was blood seeping through the hide. In another few heartbeats it was trickling down through the hair on Elk's great chest to warm the frozen ground.

'Bindings!' said Amber, desperately, looking round as if hoping to find some hanging in the air.

Bear began to untie the thong he wore round his waist, but Pearl bared her gums at him in anger and contempt.

'How are you going to bind a chest wound?' she demanded. 'He won't be able to breathe if you bind his chest!'

Amber drew in a deep wavery breath, swallowed, banished her agitation. She leant close to Elk.

'Elk, keep still, keep still, then the blood will stop flowing,' she said.

But Elk couldn't keep still because he was beginning to shiver.

'I'm cold,' he said.

Mica felt dread take hold of her. When an injured man started to shiver it was a sign he was on the way to death.

'Bring a cover,' said Amber.

Mica went quickly to the shelter. She seized the fine wolf-pelt on Elk's bed and dragged it through the hide door into the cold air.

She felt so utterly confused that she was actually dizzy. She'd thought the world was full of patterns, but where was the pattern in this? Elk and the others had gone hunting and an aurochs bull had turned on Elk and ripped open his chest. The hunter had become the hunted.

That shouldn't happen. Not when Elk was strong (Strongest), and a fine hunter, and needed by them all.

Amber took the pelt from Mica and laid it over him.

'He needs something to lie on,' said Pearl, rocking backwards and forwards, scowling and agitated. 'The ground is pulling the life-warmth out of him.'

Seal jerked his head at Mica, and she ran back into the shelter again and grabbed her own cover.

It would get covered in blood, but what did that matter if Elk died? What did anything matter? Had all the beasts of the valley somehow become filled with new cunning so they were turning against the stonemen? That mammoth had done them great damage, too, by snapping both their spears.

Seal and Bear lifted Elk onto Mica's cover. Elk let out a cry when they lifted him, and the blood began to flow very fast. Soon Mica's cover was stained. It was lucky Mica had her new tied-together furs, because . . .

. . . and then Mica did see a shape, an echo, a pattern, and the realization of what it might mean hit her so hard that she actually took a step backwards.

Her furs were tied together. Her *furs*, which were the skins of animals.

Elk was a stoneman, but he was made of meat, just like a beast.

And his torn skin was his hide.

As Mica stood, the pattern of this began to circle round her like the dizzy stars, but closer, faster, brighter. Might it be possible . . . ?

She went and found the pointed flake of flint she'd used to make holes in her wearing furs. It was a delicate thing that had been broken off during the making of an axe. She grabbed a few strands of mammoth hair, too.

No. Mammoth hair was too stiff. Her own would be better. Not ideal, but it was all she had.

She went and knelt down beside Elk and turned back his cover.

'What are you doing?' asked Garnet, sharply. *'Watch out, she has a blade!'*

Mica, pulling out a few of her longest hairs, found her wrist caught by an immensely strong hand.

'What are you doing?' demanded Seal, roughly, his black eyes glittering.

Mica looked up into them.

'I'm going to tie Elk's wound together,' she said. 'Like my furs, see?'

Garnet recoiled in horror.

'Madness!' she cried. 'Seal, the young one has run mad! Hold her!'

Seal was so strong there was no point in trying to pull away. Instead Mica looked across at Amber, willing her to understand.

'If I tie Elk's skin together then instead of one great wound there will be many small ones,' Mica said. 'And small wounds heal.'

Seal's face had gone as hard as flint.

'You will kill him,' he said. 'You will make many new wounds and that will kill him.'

'And can *you* save him?' cried Mica, in sudden frustration.

Amber drew in a long wavery breath into the silence that followed Mica's question.

'Elk will die if we do nothing,' she said.

'But it's madness!' said Garnet shrilly. '*Madness!*'

Pearl looked round the circle of them with milky eyes.

'Yes,' she agreed, though without passion. 'It's madness all right. That child has always had a touch of madness about her, and now it's coming out.'

Amber leant over Elk.

'Elk,' she began, smoothing back his hair. 'Did you hear? Mica thinks she can save you.'

'Kill him quicker, more like!' growled Seal.

There was a moment's pause. And then Elk turned to look at Amber.

'Well, if that's the choice, I reckon I'll go for the quick death,' he said, with just a ghost of humour.

And then he closed his eyes again.

Seal hesitated, looking round at them all.
'He'll die if we do nothing,' said Amber, quietly.
And Seal nodded, and made way for Mica.

Chapter 29

The only way Mica got through it was by pretending Elk's flesh wasn't alive. That helped in two ways: it gave her courage, and it helped steady her fingers.

Amber stayed with Mica, and so did Bear. They held Elk still while Mica worked, doggedly, always pretending she was doing nothing more than mending a torn pelt.

Elk gave sharp cries to begin with, and it took all Bear's strength to hold Elk still. After the third tie Elk only gasped; and after the first handful of ties his eyes rolled upwards and his limbs relaxed and he lay still as if he were dead. But he wasn't dead, because his heart kept on pumping out bright warm blood over Mica's hands.

When at last she'd finished they carried Elk carefully into the shelter, and Amber lay down beside him to give him warmth.

Mica went down to the river, broke the ice there, and washed and washed and washed until her hands were absolutely clean of the dark crusts of Elk's blood. The pieces of ice on the surface of the water tipped and turned and rocked, and then settled down and began to fuse back together again.

When she got back to the clearing she found that Bear had gone off somewhere. No one else would so much as meet her eye. Even Amber flinched a little when Mica looked in through the hide door of the shelter.

'How did you know what to do?' Amber asked. She spoke softly, but there was a wariness about her tone.

'Elk's skin . . . it looked like these pelts I tied together yesterday,' Mica said. 'It was just . . . just like an echo, I suppose.'

Amber smiled, but there was still a darkness in her eyes. A fear.

'You should not listen to echoes, Mica.'

'But they helped Elk!' said Mica, unable to believe that even now Amber hadn't changed her mind.

Elk was still asleep, so Mica left them both. Pearl was limping across the clearing towards the latrine. Her old bones always gave her pain when she walked, but she still turned her steps aside a little to avoid going near Mica.

Mica, stung, took herself out into the grass again. She looked hard for the little reindeer, but she didn't find it.

She sat amongst the grass, hurt and discouraged. Now she really had to accept that the stonemen weren't going to change. She had to accept it. Whatever new thing she discovered they weren't going to take any notice of it, no matter how valuable it was. New things frightened them. Appalled them, even.

What could she do but leave them all?

But could she really survive by herself? She would have to get some thongs, put her new hunting thing together, try it out . . .

She made her way back to the clearing. Bear was there, but even he shifted himself away from her a little when she took her place beside him to help cut up the meat for their meal.

'Why are you all shunning me?' Mica asked him, between hurt and anger. 'All I did was help Elk to stay alive!'

Bear hunched his shoulders.

'No one is shunning you,' he began; but Mica gave a snort of such scorn that he stopped what he was going to say.

He sighed, and looked round to check that no one was nearby.

'You keep talking about echoes,' he said, in a low voice.

'So?'

Bear shifted uncomfortably in his place.

'There are no echoes,' he said. 'That's just something inside your head.'

And that, of course, was true—except it was also the falsest thing Bear had ever said.

'But how can it be—'

But Bear was already shaking his head.

'People do sometimes start hearing noises when they begin to grow up,' he said. 'But you have to ignore them or they can lead you into terrible places,

Mica. Tell yourself it's just a worm in your ear. Because that's all it is.'

Bear was a fool, and these echoes, these trails of meaning, these patterns, were as real as the sky above them. She *knew* they were, because they had opened up the beauty of the world to her. She could never have imagined anything as wonderful by herself.

'The voices will fade if you want them to,' said Bear, earnestly. 'But if you carry on listening to them then they'll drive you mad with the terror of them.'

'Terror?' echoed Mica, startled despite herself.

'Stonemen have thrown themselves off cliffs, or stabbed themselves, sometimes. They've even been tricked into doing what the voices tell them and killing others of their band. *Anything* to make the voices stop.'

Mica carried on cutting through the piece of mammoth meat in front of her. She'd been sure for some time that the calls of the howlmen had some meaning. But what might that meaning be? What were they saying?

Bear raised his head and looked at her.

'Forget all these echoes,' he said, pleadingly.

'But I have just helped Elk,' was all she could say. 'And that was because of echoes. They saved Elk.'

'If he lives you'll have saved him,' said Bear. 'But what new thing will you hear next, Mica?'

And then he looked straight into her eyes and said:

'And what will it tell you to do?'

Chapter 30

Bear's words jostled uneasily in Mica's head that night. She tried to dismiss them, but her thoughts kept slipping away uncontrollably to bounce into curdling clouds and spiders' webs.

She slept at last, but woke exhausted.

Elk was still alive, but his face was as dull as his wolf-fur pelt and the skin round his wound had swollen to pull painfully against the knots Mica had made. But at least the bleeding had stopped.

Still, he was alive for the moment, which was more than anyone had hoped for, and Pearl was brewing mammoth-stomach broth to give him strength.

Seal gave his orders while they were at breakfast, for now Seal was Strongest of them all and so it was his right to be leader of the stonemen. Mica quailed at the thought. Pearl and Lynx were to stay at the shelter to look after Elk, and the others would hunt. They would make their way along the valley, keeping in touch by hand-signals. Seal went through the signals carefully, even though Mica had known them since she could walk. *Come to me. Still!*

Forward! To the axe-side! To the heart-side! Close in!

'We will kill today,' announced Seal, and Garnet gave a victory-hoot as if the words were enough to make it happen.

The wind was busy that day, but there was a brightness about the valley that gave hope of the sun burning through the mist by noon. The birds thought so too, for occasionally there would be a chirrup as clear and pure as running water, and sometimes an attempt at a snatch of song.

Mica made her way steadily through the grass. Bear was below her, with Seal in the central position, and Amber and Garnet beyond him.

And there! Bear was waving his hand. *Forward!* that meant. There must be some beast in front of them, then. Mica listened hard, but could hear nothing.

It might only be a deer. A herd of reindeer, perhaps. Or even a slinking inedible fox.

She went on cautiously, concentrating hard. That beast might be anything, and she needed above all to know where it was.

Let it be a deer, she thought. *Or a young horse*; for she couldn't help but know that Seal was fool enough to set the Men after anything. But then perhaps that was what they had to do, despite the danger, because they needed to kill, now, while the beasts were moving through the valley towards the sun. The valley would be nearly empty once winter arrived.

A low call distracted her. It wavered like an

owl's call, although it was harsher, like the juice of crowberries.

But look, Bear was signalling again. She must keep her wits about her.

Come to me!

Mica's heart started to thump. The beast must be quite close. She wished she could see it. It should be easy to see anything of any size in the wide grassland, but she knew from experience that even a horse could be invisible when its outline was cut up by the jagged tufts of the grass.

There were mounds and boulders all over the place, too, which could hide anything, even a great aurochs bull like the one that had attacked Elk yesterday. There was definitely one of those around.

Mica swallowed. Those bulls had always terrified her.

She was turning down the slope towards Bear when she did see something. She turned her head sharply, but whatever it was had gone.

What had it been? Something dark.

You got dark horses sometimes, and certainly dark deer, but . . .

She'd only got a glimpse of it, but it hadn't moved like a horse or a deer.

There it was again. Hardly more than a shadow through the mist, but . . .

. . . but yes, there was something about the thing that was more like a stoneman than any other beast. And hadn't there been a call from its direction, a low trill, just a few moments ago?

That thing was a howlman. Suddenly she was sure of it.

She almost turned aside to follow it, but she was distracted by a rustling in the grass. There was something over there. She couldn't see it, but she could hear the grass swishing against its sides. Yes: it was coming towards her.

Perhaps it was Bear. But no, it was coming too fast for anything two-footed.

And it was something heavy. Very—

—and now the ground was trembling and there, there, bursting out through the grass, was a great monster. It was putting down its horned head and charging, all in a flash of horror.

Terror froze her for an instant: and then at the last moment, when her nose was full of the stink of the thing, she suddenly realized that it was going to kill her.

She was going to die, now.

Now.

She was engulfed in an ear-splitting bellow and hot foul breath. She turned her back on it and crouched down: but she had to see it, she had to turn round and see it coming even if it was the last thing she ever—

—it was huge, hot, and she suddenly discovered that she hated it. She hated its violence, its cruelty, its destructiveness. She pulled out her axe and slashed up at it in a despairing teeth-gritted backhand . . .

. . . and then the whole hillside was toppling round her and she was falling, screaming, and something as big as an earthquake was coming down with her.

Something lashed her viciously on the leg. She tried to scream again but the air around her had gone thick and sticky and her throat was full . . .

. . . and she could no longer breathe.

Chapter 31

'*Quick!*'

A voice, but it was too far away to be important.

'*Quick, get it!*'

Mica opened her eyes, winced, and shut them again. The hard grey daylight of the snow-scraped hills was as sharp as flint. It felt as if someone was jabbing a blade into her head, too—stab—stab—stab—and when she tried to move the whole valley heaved itself sickeningly around her.

She lay still, trying to remember what had happened. She'd been hunting, and then she'd seen something up on the hillside, and then . . .

Mica frowned, trying to join her memory up to the present. She was almost sure . . .

Oh, her head *hurt*!

She was almost sure it'd been a howlman. Yes, she'd heard it calling, and then . . .

There was something dark on the ground beside her—a great gout of blood.

And then she did remember: huge powerful shoulders, and thick curved horns rising up to stab the sky.

Mica started shaking. She must have slashed right through the bull's hide as it charged her.

She swallowed, and tried to steady herself. There was no sign of any of the other stonemen, and even the faraway shouts she'd heard when she'd first opened her eyes had faded away into the distance. Of course, they'd all be chasing that great aurochs bull.

Well, the thing was wounded. She might even have slowed it down enough for the others to catch it and finish it off.

She sat quietly, and the silence grew round her. The clamour of the hunt had cleared the hills of every kind of beast. She'd make her way back to the shelter soon, but for now . . . for now she was really alone. Completely alone.

That was the strangest thing, to be alone. To have time to think. Soon her mind had begun to drift and then to fly, swooping wonderingly through the valley.

Mica wasn't sure if it was the blow to her head that was so dizzying, or whether it was all the wide space through which her mind was flying.

There was suddenly space here to think anything. To do anything.

Anything.

She untied the length of thong she wore round her waist. It was a good stout piece, longer even than she was, that had been cut in a careful spiral round and round a hide.

All right. That was the first thing. Now she needed a weight.

She found a fist-sized pebble easily enough. Tying it to the piece of thong was a struggle, but she managed it in the end.

Now. She grasped the thong by the free end and began to swing it round.

No. It was too long.

All right, hold it nearer to the pebble then.

Round and round, faster and faster until . . .

She let it go and the thing flew straight and fast, until it thumped hard into the earth.

But that wasn't quite what she needed. She needed to bring a beast down, not just hit it. Hitting it wouldn't be much good.

Mica went and retrieved the thing and found that the pebble had come off. She needed to alter it, anyway. It flew well, but it was never going to get tangled round a beast's legs.

So how . . . ?

(Perhaps Bear was right. Perhaps this was just playing games. Perhaps she was being childish, like Lynx, who always wanted to play chase or catch or tug-of-war instead of working.)

But of course: it was Lynx's playing that'd helped give her the idea in the first place! Lynx had caught hold of that thong they were stretching and they'd spun round and round until they'd spun away and fallen right on top of the bone pile.

Round and round, Mica and Lynx. Spinning.

So.

The hunting-thing felt much better once there was a pebble at either end. Mica whirled it round, and she was just getting it up to speed when one of the pebbles came loose and flew off and disappeared amongst the grass.

The fifth time this happened Mica suddenly realized someone was watching her.

She swung round in alarm—but it was only Bear. He was warm-faced, as if he'd been running.

Mica felt herself flush, too. How long had Bear been watching her? Long enough to see her hunting-thing falling to pieces, anyway.

'I didn't know you were there,' she said. It came out fiercer than she'd intended.

'I was afraid you were hurt,' said Bear.

Mica looked at Bear's glowing, kind, face. At Bear, who loved her, as long as she wasn't being who she wanted to be.

'Did you kill the bull?' she asked.

Bear shook his head.

'We nearly got it, but it was just too quick. If we'd had our long spears . . . '

Mica wound the thong back round her waist, and Bear watched her.

'Is that your hunting-thing?'

Mica shrugged.

'It doesn't work,' she admitted. 'I can't get the stones to stay on. One or the other always flies off before I'm ready to throw it.'

'Yes,' said Bear. 'I saw. What you need to do is—'

And then he broke off, standing completely still, his eyes and mouth wide as if with shock.

'What?' said Mica. 'What do I need to do?'

But he only shook his head.

'Nothing,' he said. 'Nothing. I don't know. It's just that . . . I don't know.'

But he was so distracted that Mica could hardly get a word out of him all the way back to the shelter.

Chapter 32

Amber looked ill with worry when she arrived back at the clearing.

'That bull might have killed you,' she kept saying to Mica. 'You might have been killed. What would I have done if I had lost both of you?'

Pearl pressed her lips together when she heard what had happened.

'It wouldn't have made much difference if it *had* killed her,' she said. 'We'll all be dead soon, anyway. Still,' she went on, grudgingly, 'you have to look on the bright side. That was probably the beast which tossed Elk, and the young one's given it a bleeding to avenge him. It's more than the rest of you managed.'

In the shelter Elk was propped up on a roll of furs. His face was brighter than it'd been that morning, and his wound might have looked less angry.

'Perhaps you have avenged me,' he said, and even tried to smile. 'Oh, but to think of my young one standing up to a great aurochs bull, eh? It seems only yesterday . . . '

Pearl bared her gums at him.

'Never mind yesterday,' she said. 'Our problem is tomorrow, hunter man!'

When Mica went back outside she found that Bear had warmed some broth for her.

'Here,' he said, smiling. 'It will strengthen you.'

Mica took it and sipped at it. It was good, but Seal's dark head loomed up behind Bear before she'd finished.

'There's no time to be idle,' he said. 'Mica, there's been a herd of horses through. Go and help Bear gather the dung.'

Mica and Bear worked well together. They always had. When Mica began to shiver from the cold, or from exhaustion, or perhaps from the blow to her head, Bear finished off the job more or less by himself without resenting it at all.

'All right,' said Seal, hands on hips to make himself as broad as he could. 'Now go over to the other side of the river and see if you can find any more dung there.'

Bear hesitated.

'Mica's tired, Strongest,' he said, ducking his head respectfully. 'The bull injured her.'

Seal sniffed.

'Then she needs exercise to get her strong again.'

So Mica trudged back out onto the hillside. She was soon so faint with exhaustion that she even stopped caring that she was surrounded by wild voices and bitter winds and hungry teeth.

And she hardly looked round when a low wavering call reached her, buoyed up on the shivering wind.

Chapter 33

By the next morning even Pearl was prepared to admit that there was a chance Elk wasn't going to die. Not this time.

What was certain was that for now Seal was Strongest of the stonemen.

Now Seal was in charge the days assumed a new pattern. Every day, everyone who was strong enough went out hunting from first light until dusk. Seal planned the hunts carefully and drove everyone hard, but the beasts always proved just too nimble, or just too fast, or just too far away, and they caught nothing at all. Seal's temper got sourer with every failure, and soon Lynx had learned to be very still and quiet if Seal was anywhere near.

Elk mended, but much too slowly. By the time he was going to be well enough to hunt again the valley would be empty of all but the biggest beasts, the rhino and the mammoth, which they now couldn't hope to kill.

'Yes, this will be my last winter,' said Pearl, actually rather pleased at the distinction. 'You'll be gnawing on my old bones come midwinter, you'll see.'

'No,' said Amber, distressed. 'Don't say such things. You will live to see many summers yet, old one.'

'Can't see how,' snapped Pearl, irritated to be denied this importance. 'And I'll tell you something else, woman, I reckon I'll be lucky to last until then, the way Garnet's sizing me up.'

But of course that was unthinkable. The idea that a stoneman might kill one of their old ones for meat was . . .

Well, just a few days ago it would have been unthinkable. But now that Seal was Strongest . . .

Bear only made a face when Mica told him what Pearl had said.

'Perhaps Elk will be well enough to take over again soon,' he said, glumly.

Mica had been expecting Bear to argue her out of her fears, and she was shocked again.

'But Garnet wouldn't really kill Pearl,' she began. Then stopped, uncertainly. 'Well, I know Pearl's always driven Garnet mad, but Seal wouldn't allow . . .'

And then she stopped again.

And again, Bear said nothing.

The stonemen had always been busy, but now they were hunting and hunting and hunting all day in the freezing wind, and they were all getting increasingly tired and anxious. Mica had little time to herself. She thought she heard howlmen calling once or twice but even these sounds, usually so tantalizing, even the marvellously-patterned valley itself, seemed to fade around her until all she could see was hunting, hunting, hunting.

But even hunting had its patterns, and in the long waits for beasts she had plenty of time to turn them in her mind.

She cornered Bear one evening.

'This is no good,' she told him. 'We've just *got* to start hunting in a different way.'

But Bear was already shifting his great feet as if looking for a way to escape.

She caught hold of his arm.

'Listen to me!' she said. 'I know my pebble-thing didn't work, but that doesn't mean—'

'No,' he said. 'No. It's no use, Mica.'

'But the way things are going we're going to starve! Pearl's right, isn't she? We're going to starve before the spring!'

But Bear was shaking his head.

'Forget it, Mica,' he said.

'Forget it? But this is *vital*, Bear. You must . . . you *must* understand that.'

Bear looked all round before he replied.

'I'll tell you what I do understand,' he said. 'And that's what Seal will do to you if you try telling him he's no good at hunting.'

Mica had been trying not to think about that: about suggesting to Seal that perhaps it might be possible to come up with a new idea (an *idea*!) that might work better than all his long experience as a hunter.

'But something new is the only thing that might save us!' she said, in incredible frustration.

'Really? You think that challenging Seal is going to make you live longer?' he said.

But Mica couldn't, she *couldn't* admit he was right.

'Now Seal can see the old ways aren't working he'll listen,' she said, energetically, though without believing a word of it.

'Listening is the very last thing he'll do.'

'But he must! Even Seal *must* listen!'

Bear paused, and then seemed to come to a decision. 'Mica. Look, when Elk was hurt. I was there. I saw what happened.'

Mica stared at him. Elk had been tossed by a bull. Hadn't he?

'You don't mean that Seal—'

'No. No, of course not. Seal didn't do anything. He was too slow to do anything.' But then Bear went on: 'But it's unusual, Mica, for Seal to be slow.'

Mica was too shocked to reply. To think that Seal . . .

'You know that Seal's always wanted to be Strongest,' went on Bear. 'Always. And now he is, but everything's going wrong. He's on a blade-edge, Mica, and if anyone threatens him he's going to lash out. So just how long do you think you'd last after you challenged his ability to lead the hunt?'

Mica had no answer to that.

'But . . . but I can't just give up,' she said. 'Even if we manage to kill every beast in the valley, I can't just close my eyes to what's around me. I can't stop *thinking*. Making things. Exploring.'

'But we're stonemen,' said Bear, earnestly. 'That's who we are. New ideas are tempting, but we have to follow our Strongest, and we have to be true to our band. We can't . . . we can't be anything different, any more than we can grow wings and fly away.'

Mica stared at him despairingly. He'd never understand. Never.

'But that's what an idea is, Bear,' she said. 'It's a pair of wings to help us fly away.'

But he didn't understand that, either.

Chapter 34

Elk was getting stronger. Pearl inspected his wound every day, but didn't touch it.

'It heals itself,' she said, slightly disappointed. 'There's no need to rub good bull-snot on that.' She put her nose close to the wound and sniffed hard. 'Not a sign of rot, either,' she went on, put-out. 'Though perhaps my old nose is failing. Mica, you have a sniff!'

Mica advanced cautiously and sniffed delicately at the bruised skin.

'Well?' demanded Pearl.

'It smells all right to me.'

Pearl pulled down the corners of her mouth.

'Well, it looks as if he's going to live, then,' she said, grudgingly. 'It was only a flesh wound, after all. Hardly touched the meat, though his blood flowed quickly. That'll be because of his fear, of course.'

'Then I'm surprised there wasn't a fountain as high as a man!' said Elk, without ill-feeling.

Pearl snickered a laugh.

'It's a pity you weren't *more* scared,' she said jeeringly. She was so old she feared no one. 'If you'd been a bit more frightened you might have had the wit to get out of the way of the bull's horn.'

Then she turned and hobbled away, still cackling. It was a long time since Pearl had been able to move faster than one of the others, and she meant to make the most of it.

Elk tucked his furs back in warmly, wincing as he touched his wound.

'I'm sorry,' said Mica, helplessly. Now the stonemen were heading towards starvation she was discovering how much they meant to her.

He looked up at her in surprise.

'Oh no,' he said. 'Oh no, this wound has worked out very well for me. Oh, but it has,' he went on, seeing her confusion. 'We all knew Seal was going to challenge me before long, and this way I've come out with my limbs and my dignity intact. Oh yes. It's given me time to think, too, you know. I've never really had time to think much before. Not properly.' He looked up at her with berry-bright eyes. 'Being Strongest means always being ready, Mica. Always knowing what to do. You never have time to worry about anything further away than tomorrow.'

'Well, Seal doesn't even know what to do for tomorrow,' said Mica, bitterly.

Elk took in a breath as if to laugh, but it ended up as a grimace of pain.

'Seal will be all right,' he said at last. 'Don't you worry about Seal. I'll soon have him sorted out.

He'll do anything as long as he thinks he's decided it himself. Especially if he thinks it'll annoy me.'

Mica was really startled by his cunning.

'I'm not sure Seal *can* think,' was all she said.

Elk put a scarred and calloused hand over hers.

'He's not like you,' he agreed. 'But then no one is. What you've done for me is marvellous. Truly marvellous.'

'But mad.'

Elk shrugged.

'Perhaps. Garnet thinks so, that's for sure, and what she thinks Seal thinks too.'

That was true enough. Seal would do nothing without Garnet's approval.

'I've had an idea for hunting,' Mica said, suddenly. 'It's mad, and it doesn't really work. But if we could find out how to make the thing hold together we'd be able to kill deer. Horses, too. I think we'd be able to get ourselves enough meat for the whole winter. But the thing is, Seal and Garnet are never going to let us try it out. So we're all going to die.'

Elk didn't say anything for a while.

'Well,' he said at last. 'Seal is Strongest, young one.'

'But—'

He smiled.

'Always *but*. It always was. Some of the others wanted all those *buts* crushed out of you, Mica, but I always thought there was a lot of strength behind your *buts*. Yes, and I can see I was right, there. There's a lot of strength in you, Mica.'

153

She was going to say *but* again, but he held up a hand to stop her.

'You're right, of course,' he went on. 'There are too many of us to survive on our stores. But do you know something? *Too many* is the one thing you've got a chance of sorting out.'

He held her hand tightly for a moment, and then he yawned hugely and settled himself down to sleep.

Mica felt puzzled, but also comforted by Elk's words. What could he mean but that she should leave the stonemen? That he had faith that somehow she'd be able to find a way to stay alive?

It seemed that everything was telling Mica to leave. Being here was crushing the life out of her, mind and body, that was for certain.

Well, she must remember that Elk had faith in her, and she must never forget that the world was full of marvels. She didn't yet know how she could survive, but that knowledge might come, in time, if she carried on searching for it.

So she must carry on searching.

Even though with Seal around that was going to be perilous.

Chapter 35

Seal was Strongest: he owned every moment of Mica's time, and every particle of her strength, and so from that moment Mica became a thief. She seized every smallest chance to think. She observed everything in the valley carefully, looking for links, for strands of possibility, for a way to join one thing to another and make a path to something new.

Seal was always watchful—always suspicious—but there were a handful of chinks of time in every day that could be used if only Mica was daring enough. If she went hunting she was quite often out of sight of the others, and if she was cutting reeds then surely no one would notice if she spent a finger's-width of the sun playing with the reeds before she brought them home.

'Bones,' said Seal to Mica one morning. 'The mammoth. Bring them.'

The mammoth was only a skeleton, now. Most of its bones were frozen into the ice, but Mica managed to lever a few ribs free. The skull was too massive to think of moving, but . . .

. . . but of course! *The mammoth's skull!*

She had to use her axe, but it didn't take so very long to get one of the side teeth out of the jawbone. Of course a mammoth tooth was no use to the stonemen. It was a treasure, all the same. Or might be.

The thing wasn't easy to carve. Mica had planned to make a reindeer, but she broke the head off almost at once. But then she discovered that the bit that was left looked a little like a bear, and soon after that she got the hang of using a flake of flint to scrape away the ivory.

Mica had no idea why she was making the thing, but she became obsessed with it. Every moment she could snatch from under Seal's suspicious eyes she spent working on the little bear.

The thing was turning out to have a great fat belly: well, perhaps it was a she-bear about to cub. Mica imagined the tiny ivory cubs, all clambering and squeaking and warm, and—

—and she was halfway across the clearing before she knew what had hit her. She landed hard on her stomach. She was trying to drag some air back into her lungs when she sensed Seal above her. She pushed herself sideways, but another great blow caught her shoulder and pushed her face into the frozen ground.

She kicked out and one of her feet made contact with something. That gave her just enough time to roll onto her back.

Above her, Seal's face was blank with rage.

He's going to kill me, she thought.

'Strongest!'

That was Bear's voice, but Seal showed no sign of hearing him. He raised a great fist.

He's going to kill me, Mica thought again—and suddenly believed it. Seal was going to kill her.

'*Strongest!*'

Seal's eyes never even flickered. He took in a great breath and focused all his strength in his arm. Mica put up her own arms to save herself, even though she knew that Seal would break her bones like twigs.

But then someone threw itself towards Seal and grabbed Seal's mighty arm, grabbed it and hung on grimly like a wolf attacking a bear, no matter how violently Seal tried to shake him off.

Seal let out a great bellow of wrath and he forgot Mica. Mica saw what was going to happen and screamed *no!* but it did no good. Seal's fist hit home on Bear's back with a dreadful hollow sound and suddenly Bear was down, rolling and scrambling and getting up again like lightning, but not quite quick enough to get right out of reach. A great swinging punch caught Bear on the side of the head and sent him flying to land sprawling across the hearth.

The fire! Bear was in the embers of the fire and nothing burned so quickly as furs. Oh, but Bear would—

Seal grabbed Bear by the furs at his throat and pulled him up. Seal's face was set in a grimace of fury. He gave a great roar and picked Bear up bodily, higher and higher, until Seal's hands were at full stretch above his head. And then he was hurling him into the waving grass. The effort of that put Seal off-balance for a moment. He staggered, and put up a hand to his shaggy head: and then from the entrance to the shelter came a long low whistle of awe.

It cut through the horror and the fury of the scene like a knife through flesh.

'Well, I've never seen anything to match that,' said Elk, shaking his head in admiration. 'The power of that throw! You have the strength of a mammoth, Strongest, and no doubt about it.'

Seal stood, taking in great rasping gasps. The blindness of his rage seemed to be fading, but Mica still didn't dare move a muscle.

Elk was standing in the doorway of the shelter. He was bent forward a little so as not to pull at the ties in his wound. He must have moved fast when he heard the commotion outside, even though it was far from easy for Elk to move fast.

It wasn't easy for him to laugh, either, but now he did that, too.

'Well, we can all feel safe with a Strongest with that much power in his arms,' he said cheerfully. 'We're well set up, now, our band is.'

Seal wiped his brow with the back of his hand. His face was still set in a scowl.

'Bear,' he snarled. 'Here.'

Bear's nose was bleeding, and he was cradling one of his arms. He paused for just a moment as he reached the edge of the grass and then he walked steadily over to where Seal stood. Mica could hardly believe that anyone could have such courage.

'Who is Strongest?' demanded Seal.

Bear went down on his knees, as if he'd been beaten in a challenge.

'Seal is Strongest,' he said.

Seal stood for a few heartbeats, his chest heaving. Then he kicked Bear in the stomach just hard enough to knock him over, and strode away.

Amber was there swiftly, helping him up, testing his limbs for damage.

'I'm all right,' he kept saying thickly. 'It's nothing. I'm all right.'

Mica hardly dared look at him. All this was her fault.

She went and got a piece of fine deer hide and began to wipe the blood away from his nose.

'I'm sorry,' she said. 'I'm sorry. I didn't know Seal was close.'

Bear winced a little as she caught a tender place.

'Seal is always close,' he said heavily, and closed his eyes.

Mica searched the whole clearing for the mammoth-tooth bear, but she couldn't find it. Had it spun off into the grass? Or had someone picked it up?

It didn't make any difference, anyway. She wouldn't have dared work on it any more. Bear was right. Seal was always close, and the smallest step away from the ways of the stonemen might be enough to make him kill her.

Bear was right.

Except for one thing. Seal couldn't really kill her: for being here meant that most of her was already dead.

Chapter 36

The stonemen had been out all day again, and now the evening mist was rising to meet the dusk.

Soon Seal would call an end to another useless hunt and lead the way back to the shelter.

'Mica,' said Amber, softly, appearing out of the mist and making Mica jump.

Mica had hardly spoken to anyone for days. Seal's eyes were constantly watchful and she hardly dared open her mouth at all in case Seal suspected some plot. In any case, there was little to say. She felt as if she hardly existed, now, so how could she be friends with anyone, even Bear who'd saved her?

'I know things are difficult at the moment,' said Amber, speaking quietly even though out here in the freezing mist of the hillside there was surely no chance of their being overheard. 'But I don't like to see you avoiding Bear. You've always been such friends. He's growing into a fine young man, too. He'll be missing you very much.'

Would he? Yes, of course he would. Except, of course, that it wasn't *her* Bear would miss. Not Mica as she wanted to be, as she needed to be, as she should be, in any case.

'Bear's just like the rest of you,' Mica said at last. 'He doesn't want me to . . . to be myself. And I can't stop doing that. I can't stop . . . '

'Thinking,' said Amber, sadly.

Mica gave her a sharp glance. Amber could hardly know what thinking was. Oh, but Mica just wanted to get up and walk and walk, over the hills and far away, until she got to . . .

. . . but who knew where she might get? Perhaps if she only went on long enough she might even catch up with the summer.

'This valley. It is wonderful, you know,' said Amber, suddenly. 'The swell of the hills and the running of the water. Even the cold. It is wonderful.'

That surprised Mica even more, for the cold was the first enemy of the stonemen. That was something even Mica had never questioned.

Amber smiled dreamily.

'The howlmen have always come with the cold,' she went on. 'Always with the cold. When I was young I used to think their calls were made of ice because they made me shiver whenever I heard them.'

What? But what could *Amber* know about howlmen?

'Their voices are so strange,' Amber went on. 'Heart-quickening, like clouds or moonlight shadows. The other stonemen never seemed to hear them properly, but I did. I loved to hear them, even though the others told me they were nothing. I used to long for quiet in case I missed their voices in all the clatter of work. And then one day . . . '

Mica, terrified that Amber would stop, hardly dared breathe.

'It was long ago,' Amber went on, softly. 'When Elk and I were beginning to be more than friends. Elk was always kind, you know. He was very like Bear, except that Elk was never quiet. No, Elk was always full of noise and laughter.'

'But then one day . . . ' prompted Mica; and Amber sighed.

'But then one day I was at the shelter alone. I can't remember why. But there I was, all alone. And a howlman started to call not far away.'

'Were you afraid?' whispered Mica.

Amber laughed, as if the very idea was ridiculous.

'Why should I have been afraid?' she asked. 'You know what the calls of the howlmen are like: thrilling, and harsh as bee-stings, and sweet as honey . . . yes,' she said, thoughtfully, 'for a while I felt as if I were floating in a river of honey. The calling came closer and closer until, oh, I was pierced with the sound of it. And a shadow came with it. Something impossible. A creature that could only be a dream. And for a while the dream filled me with such a mixture of pain and happiness as I had never imagined.'

Amber's face was filled with a longing, a sort of joy, that Mica had never seen there before.

'And then?' breathed Mica.

Amber took a deep breath.

'And then I was alone again. Completely *completely* alone. It was terrible. I thought I would die of loneliness. But then the stonemen came back hungry, and Elk was amongst them. And I knew that though Elk would never carry me to the centre of a river of honey, he would never leave me completely alone. And so I stopped listening to the howlmen. And now I don't even hear them any more.'

Mica wasn't sure she understood. There was something hugely important in this story, but she wasn't certain what it was.

'You were born the next autumn,' went on Amber, suddenly matter-of-fact. 'A little earlier than we were expecting; and that, of course, was why you were so little and thin.'

Mica had always been skinny and long-limbed. *Unhealthy*, Pearl called her, because her dark skin never glowed, though Mica was seldom ill. But Mica certainly wasn't stout and round-chested like the other stonemen.

So what was Amber saying? A howlman had visited her . . . and Mica had been born the next autumn, earlier than they had expected.

So did that mean . . .

Mica looked searchingly at Amber, but Amber was shaking her head.

'That's all I know,' she said. 'That's all I know, Mica, truly; except that I have always loved you, and

Elk has always loved you, too, and that we have never had any more young ones.'

She turned to look round her at the white wisps of mist that were rising from the frozen hillside and she said it again, wistfully.

'That's all I know.'

Chapter 37

Sleep did not come to Mica that night—but then she hardly expected it to, for lately the darkness only seemed to waken her, to start her mind running and racing just when the other stonemen were becoming dull and ready for sleep. She lay listening to the snores of the others and thought about Amber's story: about the look of joy on Amber's face when she had told it, and about how the joy had turned to sadness when she had said *now I don't hear them any more.*

A howlman had come and filled Amber with joy, but then it had left her, and that had been terrible: something precious lost for ever.

For ever.

Mica turned carefully on her bed.

Even Elk seemed to be asleep. His wound was healing so well that Pearl was already talking about taking out the ties that Mica had put into his skin.

Elk had been Strongest for a long time—more than ten seasons, it must be. He would never challenge Seal, now, but would submit to him and become a crafty, skilled, contriving member of the band. A power by the hearth, strong but never noticed.

Yes, Seal would rule the stonemen and Garnet would stand behind him and they would all stumble on until their food ran out. And all because they had never listened to the howlmen, had never felt that moment of lightness, of joy, of connectedness with the whole world from the dark river to the sparkling stars. All because they had never realized that the whole world was moving constantly, and that they must move with it.

All because they thought their lives were complete. That they were all they could ever be.

Mica, restless, sat up. Her breath formed dim plumes of frost through the air, but the cold only seemed to waken her even more, to make her feel more alive.

The stonemen were breathing softly all round her. The stonemen, who were her family, her workmates, her everything.

But it was no good. If by any chance she lived through this long winter then soon there'd be another one, and another, until she became worn and tired; or worn and spiteful; or worn and bitter.

And what would happen to the joy which had illuminated Amber's face then?

If Mica stayed with the stonemen . . .

Those howlmen understood about new things. They probably understood things Mica had never even dreamed of.

Bear said they were cruel. Killers.

Oh, but what other chance was there for her but to go and find the howlmen? She couldn't, she *couldn't* live alone. What choice was there, but between one danger and another?

Mica was careful not to disturb anyone as she got up. Bear coughed a little when she stepped over him, but he soon settled back to his snoring.

Mica slipped through the hide door and made her way softly across the clearing.

There might be lions waiting in the grass, but she had no time to be afraid.

That was really true. She *had no time*.

She pushed on through the chilly dark.

She was in search of something wonderful, before it was too late.

Chapter 38

The valley was dark, but not as dark as the inside of the shelter had been. The trodden earth glimmered a little even though the moon was hidden, and the scanty scraps of snow had the pale gleam of toadstools.

Mica stood listening. Nothing, except for the busy bustling wind.

She went softly across the clearing. She didn't know exactly where she had to go, or if she would ever be coming back: but the end of her journey was going to be somewhere wonderful, all the same.

Mica paused as she reached the track which led down to the river. This valley was home to many creatures: apart from the horses and deer and mammoth there were wolves, and the hyenas which emerged silently from the grass within an hour of any kill; and sometimes there would be a solitary scrawny lion slinking its way after them.

Well, hyenas and lions were cowards, for all their knife-like teeth: Bear had shown her that. Yes, she had learned courage, now. All you had to do was stand up as tall as you could and put your arms high in the air and scream, and they would run away.

Mica wished the wind was not so strong, though. The grass was almost rattling in the icy gusts, and she might not hear a stalking lion.

Not until it was too late.

Mica stood, wavering, between fear and longing, and as she did the clouds slid clear of the crescent moon and its cool light spilled gleaming over the valley. Grass, mounds, hollows, the milky streak of the icy river, all grey-glittering before her.

And in the wake of the moon came the stars, more than anyone could count, piercing the night, sharp as fire or ice.

And she had never seen anything so marvellous.

She cast aside all fear and began to run.

The river was almost completely ice, now, with hardly a trickle of water to twist and sparkle in the moonlight. Mica turned along beside it, heading through the luminous darkness towards the pool where she'd seen the dark, fur-clad, extraordinary figure of the howlman. It would hardly still be there, of course, but still she ran, feeling as if she could never tire, and the hills ran along on either side of her, familiar, yet utterly alien.

She ran on beside the river under the light of the waning moon and the distant hosts of stars. She was glad of the light they shed because she was searching for something.

It was next to impossible there should be any tracks left after all this time, she knew that, but . . .

This was the right place, anyway, where the river made a wide bend that slowed the current and formed the pool. It was always the first place where the river froze.

The ice creaked under her feet, but Mica pushed her way between the dusty tops of the bulrushes and across to the other bank.

Where had it been? Where had it been, that howlman who had carved the tiny reindeer? Was it here, or over . . .

And there, gleaming, in a place where the swollen spring river had gouged an overhang into the soil, lay a piece of fine sharp flint.

Mica picked it up. It was gleaming. Recently worked.

That howlman had run away through the reeds when Bear had frightened it, and it had left a track, after all: a trail of bent and broken stems.

Mica didn't move for a long time. She found herself full of fear, but of excitement, too.

Here was a path to a new world. A world that wasn't stubbornly unchanging like the world of the stonemen. A world where new thoughts, new *worlds* were being created all the time.

For a moment the thought of all those new paths to unknown places made her dizzy.

But if she followed the trail of broken reeds, if she found the howlman, wouldn't it kill her at once?

Or would it recognize that she was a creature much like itself?

It was mad even to think of trying it. Perilous.

At the end of the path of broken reeds she found a path. She didn't know where it would lead, or what she was going to do when she got to the end of it, but she took it anyway.

Soon the path was rising before her into strange hills which might hide anything.

(Even Bear, kind, foolish, brave Bear, had been terrified of that little scraggy howlman.)

Well, she could still turn back. Go back and be safe with Elk and Amber and Pearl. Do what she was told; do what needed to be done. Hunt and hunt and hunt and hope. Scrape the hides and break the scum of ice on the stock pond and chew food for Pearl.

She could even stop listening to the calls of the howlmen. Amber had shown her that.

And, after all, Amber was not really unhappy.

Was she?

From somewhere ahead of her, faintly, Mica heard a calling. It was a little like howling, or a bird's call, except that it went on and on; and now she recognized the shape of it as it rose and fell through the cold air. It was like a shadow of a shadow of a shadow of the patterns of the stars; or perhaps of the pattern of life; or of death.

Mica went forward more quickly. Now a second voice had joined in the calling. The sound rose in waves through the air. It was nothing near as beautiful as the stars in the sky above her: in some ways it wasn't really very much different from a beast's calling.

Yes. This was far from the glory of the patterns of the stars; it was more like the pattern of the earth and the beasts and the summer grass which shone and shivered as she passed.

At long last, after much climbing, Mica reached the top of the dark hillside and found herself looking down into the dark folds of a new valley. She stood and gazed. Gazed and gazed.

There was a fire far below her, flickering with a leaping warmth like a sinking sun. It illuminated a small circle and showed her . . .

. . . yes, there was a shelter down there, but it wasn't built against a landslip, but stood alone in the middle of a clearing.

But how could that happen? How did it stand up? How on earth could such a thing *stand up*?

And look, there were a handful of creatures by the fire. Howlmen. One of them was working at something it held in its hand, and as it worked its mouth was moving. This must be one of the ones who were making the swooping, soaring noise.

The earth-patterned noise.

Mica could not understand any of the words in their calling, but she could hear it was full of joy: full of things they couldn't hold in their hands.

It was not really beautiful, but it made her heart beat fast; filled her with a marvellous excitement.

And even though those were howlmen, cruel howlmen, who might kill her when they saw her, she had to know what they knew. She had to learn, change, enter the new worlds that the howlmen's calling opened to her, grasp this chance to live her life as fully as she could.

Even if it meant her life was going to be very very short.

Chapter 39

Mica made her way down the slope towards the shelter of the howlmen. She slipped once or twice, but the wind was whipping the grass and it hid the sound of her falling.

She came to a stop at the edge of their clearing, before the howlmen's fire could light a betraying spark in her eye.

The group of howlmen were moving, getting up and going to stand in a ring round the fire. They weren't calling any more, but were speaking to each other (though they weren't using proper words so Mica couldn't understand what they were saying). Mica pulled her head covering across her face so only her eyes were uncovered. These creatures, these howlmen, were full of power, and she was filled with terror and amazement.

Now they had begun to call again, all of them: so many lines of sound, dipping and soaring. The sound of it was sharp, somehow, sharp enough to pierce Mica through to her bones; though there was no pain and no blood, but only an endless fear and wonder.

The creatures had begun to move. They were pacing steadily, carefully, keeping time with the pulses and surges of their calls. Sometimes a howlman would take a step backwards, or turn to one side, or sway as the grass sways on a mild day, or leap high through the flickering air.

Their movements were echoing the patterns of their voices, Mica suddenly realized. Their steps made it visible, sketched the pattern of the sounds onto the air.

Oh, and it was irresistible. Mica found herself swaying to the beat of the howlmen. The voices alone filled her with yearning, but these movements were setting fire to every particle of her body. It was so wonderful, so powerful, *so strong*, that her mind could hardly bear it. She wanted to close her eyes and clasp her hands over her ears to block it all out; and yet she would not have missed a single instant of it to save her life.

Now a single voice was rising clear and high. A female's voice. It floated over the warm flames of the fire, solemn and slow and yet full of strength.

There she was. That one, slim and dark. The others had stepped back to leave her alone by the fire. She was moving gently, gracefully as a deer, holding up her arms as she called, her head tipped back to the stars. This was a . . . a reaching, a longing, perhaps even a grasping. It spoke in every limb.

Mica suddenly couldn't bear it. That creature was speaking to the stars: treading their patterns with her body. That was what Mica had longed for, and yet she was still outside it all, squatting in the cold darkness with the sound sending shivers of yearning through her blood.

She couldn't bear it. She *couldn't*. There must be some way to bridge this dreadful gap so that she, too, could speak to the stars.

She rose cautiously to her feet. The howlmen were watching the female as she moved in the firelight, light as a hawk in a summer breeze, and they never turned their heads.

Mica felt awkward to begin with. Her arms were stiff, and her feet were always a little behind the beat of that sweetly buoyant line of sound.

But it became easier as she went on. She took slow soft steps, then quick ones, then stopped and turned. Soon the other howlmen's voices joined in with the female's, creating a web of sound which made Mica's steps easier still, until the sounds were flowing through her body, sending it stepping and spinning and reaching.

Leg and toe, arm and hand, chin and neck and back. The air in the valley was cold as ice, but her blood was rushing hot with excitement and her heart was thumping to the beat of the sound that was surrounding her, piercing her, drawing her on. Oh, this was nearer flying than walking; near being the wind. Yes, it was like being the wind, because around her the world had begun to fade, to get dimmer as if with the distance, until hardly a shadow of it was left in her mind.

And at last Mica was free of the knowledge that there were beasts to hunt and skins to clean. She was free, free of all the endless struggling to live so that more beasts could be hunted and more skins cleaned.

She slipped free even of time, as a snake from its skin, and she was here, now, under the crystals of the stars that sent fragments of rainbows through the gleaming ice that surrounded the circle of the fire.

Mica raised her face to the sky. The wind had swept it clean and the stars shone above her like her name, like mica, in a thousand glints of light. And as she looked and stepped and turned she saw the pattern, or heard the pattern, or felt the pattern in the stars. And she realized that she, like the creatures by the firelight, was obeying it with foot and mind and voice.

Outside time, and outside the world, Mica gloried in the patterns of the stars.

Chapter 40

Mica traced the patterns of the stars with her feet, with her arms, with her fingers, and the voices of the howlmen pierced her with delight. She stepped and leapt and turned, careful and yet carefree, while the sky turned above her.

But then suddenly the trail of sound dissolved into the air, and Mica was left stranded and gasping. The star-patterns faded and faded, until the stars were no more than tiny points of distant light and the harshness of the freezing air was closing round Mica again.

Mica lowered her arms, full of dismay. These creatures could conjure up the patterns of the stars: they had knowledge which could transform everything, which could turn the whole world into something marvellous.

But now they had stopped and she was left in the darkness, and alone.

The howlmen were all back in the circle of firelight, now, and their steps had quickened to a run. Their voices were deeper, too, and although Mica could understand none of the words she could feel the determination of them, the force behind them.

This was hunting. She recognized that at once. This was coming in a band to chase a beast to the death. *Death*, they called, and she understood the word even though the word was different from her own. *Death*. Again and again it came. *Death*.

Mica dropped down and made herself as small as she could. Hunting and death had always been part of her life, of course, because without death there could be no life for the stonemen. But the power of this sent her heart thumping and her breath juddering inside her chest.

Now above the deep repeated call of *death* there were other voices, blaring, triumphant. The howlmen began to stamp and punch the air, bellowing steam through the shadows.

Mica could not look away, even though the lines of sound were like snakes, cunning and strong. She found herself actually cowering. Oh, she could understand this. In the calls she could see the points of the howlmen's spears gleaming and feel the bodies of the howlmen warm with eagerness. They were going to kill, to kill, to kill . . .

Mica suddenly clasped her hands to her ears. This was only a hunting expedition, but the horror of it was worming its way darkly into her mind. Just as the stars in that female's voice had filled her with amazement and joy, these voices were also pulling her into the howlmen's world. She could feel the pulse of the hunters' hearts as they crept on through the pale grass.

And there, there! There was the prey! It was running, running, running for its life, but the howlmen were cunning and there would be no escape.

The prey knew it, too. It was turning at bay. The howlmen were looking into its terrified eyes, and Mica was looking with them, and—

—and it was Mica.

It was *Mica*. *She* was the prey.

The spears were closing in, surrounding her. They were stabbing, stabbing, and the triumph of the howlmen was swooping around her as blood pulsed from her wounds.

Mica was caught, and she could hardly breathe. She was dying.

With her last breath she opened her mouth and she screamed.

Chapter 41

Mica's scream split the invisible air of the valley of the howlmen—and in that instant, horror upon horror, she realized what she'd done.

The howlmen's voices broke off abruptly. The vision their voices had called into being vanished instantly. And then a new hunt began.

The tallest of the howlmen gave a shout and waved his arm in a gesture Mica had always known: *after the beast!* And this time Mica really was the beast.

Mica squirmed round, pushed herself to her feet, and fled.

The hillside was dark, but there were stars sprinkled across the sky and the sharp moon would betray Mica if it found its way out from the clouds. She half ran, half scrambled, up the steep hill through the frozen grass. The howlmen were shouting behind her. She could hear they'd spread out: there was no chance of her turning back and slipping past them.

She threw herself on desperately, stumbling and running and stumbling again. Her breath was coming fast, now, and there was sweat forming under her furs.

Even the air seemed warmer, and the wind smoother, not so fussy.

That should have warned her what was going to happen. But it didn't: the brightness of the howlmen's death-calls was in her head and she could think of nothing but running, but running, but running.

There was a shout almost beside her, terrifyingly close. She swerved away and almost ran into another of the howlmen. Or perhaps it was a beast, she couldn't be sure because suddenly she couldn't *see*, and she might blunder into anything.

But why couldn't she see? Was it that the bright blood of the howlmen's calling was still dazzling her, or was it that the looming hill in front of her was cutting off the sky?

Or was this what blind panic was like?

More shouts, some to her axe-side, some to her heart-side.

Here. A mound. It was steep, but she couldn't risk turning aside. Up, up, up to the top and then stop for a moment to cast a hasty glance around—

—and to discover that ahead of her, above the high black ridge, all the stars had gone out.

Chapter 42

Mica gaped at the great black bank of cloud that was advancing on her. Here was a darkness to hide her from her enemies, but here also was a force to sweep her away like a gnat, to destroy her in a hand's-breadth passage of the moon.

But there were hunters behind her, so only one way she could go. Mica gathered her wits and threw herself onwards, towards the storm.

The blizzard hit her with an unbelievable suddenness. The charcoal hill ahead of her went black, real true black, and a low moaning roar rushed up on her. It mounted to a fierce squall and then suddenly a scoop of wind had blown back her head covering and flakes of wind-whirled ice were flinging themselves at her to freeze on her lips.

She ducked away from the onslaught, but that turned her towards her hunters. That was no good. She had to fight her way on against the storm.

Her furs were shuddering and shivering and flapping round her. This strom would soon kill her if the howlmen didn't. She needed shelter.

She bent her head down and began to force her way into the roaring, snow-whirling blizzard.

Oh, but it was black. She tried not to flinch away from the driving snow, but it wasn't long before she wasn't even sure where the brow of the hill was, or which way the ground was sloping under her feet.

She stopped, turned round once, and then again. She pushed down the panic that was rising inside her and forced herself forward. Particles of snow stung her eyes but she went on as best she could, with the wind howling, howling around her in dizzying snowy gusts and buffets. At least the howlmen would give up their hunt, now, and go back to their shelter and safety. Nothing could live long in this.

The snow was soon up to her ankles, and soon after that she found herself floundering in a drift nearly up to her knees. She went on doggedly, even though it was hard to stop herself flinching away from the spinning snow. She was completely lost, not even sure whether she was back over the brow of the hill and into her own valley. She was afraid of walking into a herd of aurochs, and she was afraid of blundering onto the ice of the river and falling through to a black and choking death.

She had to find shelter, so . . .

. . . but she could hardly think at all with all this noise around her. The wind was like a great host of invisible beasts, pushing and jostling her until she was too buffeted to be sure of anything. The screaming cold was filling her mind.

She stopped, confused, then stumbled on again, lashed by the vicious flecks that came at her out of the darkness.

Stopped again. Stumbled on.

Stopped.

Stopped.

But she mustn't stop. She must keep going, keep going, even though she was afraid she'd got turned round in the darkness and was now heading away into the hills. The slashing snow was swirling round and round her, up and round and vanishing into the darkness, so she couldn't even be sure which way the wind was blowing any more.

But whatever she did she mustn't stop. Go on, go on.

Oh, but the snow was cruel. It found its way through her furs and stuck to her skin, leaching her life-heat out of her. Oh, and she didn't want to die. Not yet. Not when there was still so much to discover.

The snow was often past her knees, now: the blizzard was so vast it felt as if it was even greater than the hills themselves.

And she was so tiny, so frail, compared with all this.

But she must keep going anyway. If necessary she must keep going all through the—

—her foot caught something and she fell headlong. She landed and found the snow soft, whipped by the wind to a feathery lightness that was hardly more substantial than the air. She lay for a moment, amazed to find it so gentle, so comfortable, after all the confusion and freezing misery of trying to force her way against it.

(No. No, this was wrong, wrong, wrong. It was hard for Mica to think because most of her mind was filled with surprise at the warmness of the snow, but this was *wrong*. Snow was cold, bitter, painful: she shouldn't be filled with this drowsy warmth. She *couldn't* be.)

She put her head down on the snow anyway. She would rest for just a little while, just a moment, until she got her breath back. Or perhaps she would wait until tomorrow, when the wind had died down, to find her way back.

And as she finally relaxed there was a sudden lull in the howling of the wind and she heard something. An echoing. A chirruping.

Like fragments of ice dropping into deep water, or onto stone.

Mica startled, looked up, but as soon as she did some fluke of the wind flung a whirlwind of snow into her face. And it was bitter and cruel again, and there was no comfort here after all.

With a great effort she pushed herself to her knees and then to her feet. She stood, swaying, with the wind howling round her and the snow whipping and turning and soaring until sky and earth and air together were tumbling round her and she seemed hardly more than a snowflake amidst it all.

But she *was* more than a snowflake. She was *Mica*.

She wiped away the snowflakes that had stuck to her eyelashes and pushed herself painfully onwards.

It was so cold now it was hard to breathe. Perhaps her blood was thickening and soon her heart would freeze.

But she went on, anyway. Even if she died, she would die searching.

Mica didn't know how long she forced her way through the dark and dizzying snow. Sometimes she fell, but the shrill cries that came with the wind were always enough to bring her to her feet again.

Once she even found herself calling back to it. *What do you want with me?* she called, as if the storm were alive, as if the howling came from some living thing. This mighty storm had blown the whole of Mica's world adrift, so that it seemed not impossible that there were real voices calling amongst the screaming wind: not howlmen voices, but voices clear and cold as icicles, cruel as frost, shining as the invisible stars. Once she might even have felt a freezing hand run itself lingeringly down her cheek.

But all that could only be some sort of snow-madness, of course. It was to be welcomed, anyway, because it made the world seem less vast and formless, and gave her the courage to keep on even when the wind mounted again into such a great shrieking howl that for a moment it seemed as if the whole valley had taken flight around her.

At last (perhaps after hours, for Mica had lost all track of time) she fell again, and this time she stayed where she fell, too tired even to care about the wind-voices around her. She hardly had the strength to turn her head so she could breathe.

But when at last she did, she saw something ahead of her. A low mound, black against the luminous charcoal of the snow.

She pushed herself up yet again.

Chapter 43

It was a strange thing, that mound. It was less than a stoneman in height, and only a couple of stonemen in length. But there was something unnatural about it, something that told Mica it wasn't just a heaving up of the earth of the valley.

She crawled towards it. The snow was vicious, swiping at her eyes, but she was sure . . . yes, there was a crack in the snow that covered the mound. It looked as if it might be big enough to get through.

Her mind was numbed by the cold and the fury of the storm, or she would never have crawled through that opening into the unknown darkness.

The inside was pitch black, but something in the sound of her breathing told Mica the mound was hollow. She crawled forward a little way. The floor of the place was cluttered with . . . she didn't know what they were, but they might have been great bones.

She stopped and brushed the snow off her face. The storm was still whooping and howling outside but this place was absolutely still. The relief of getting

190

out of the storm was tremendous, but it was as if she'd crawled right out of the world and left half her senses behind. Sight, hearing, touch (her hands felt heavy and quite lifeless) were diminished or vanished altogether.

But at least she could breathe, and she could thrust her frozen useless hands into her furs to warm some life back into them.

The place was ice cold, of course, but Mica began to feel her senses returning to her. Whatever this place was, she could rest here.

She crawled further away from the opening. The place was low and narrowed very quickly. As soon as she found space on the floor she curled up, tucking her hands into the dry glutton fur under her chin, and lay still.

When she awoke she found she could see a soft grey light. She sat up, not quite sure where she was. Not quite sure if she were still alive.

Through the opening in the side of the mound she could see that the snow was hardly falling any more, but sliding lazily through the air in great loops and twists. The wind was definitely much quieter, too: still blustery, but no longer shrieking or howling.

The light of the dawn spilled through the opening to the mound. She'd been right, the floor of the place was covered in a jumble of bones. Huge bones that must be from some long-dead mammoth.

Mica felt a sudden pang of pity for the beast they'd killed. Had its hunted heart thumped as hard in its ribs as hers had done?

But now at least she knew where she was. This mound was the carcass of the mammoth that had died so long ago up on the far hillside. The snow had clogged the gaps between its ribs and made a place just big enough for a poor shivering creature to find shelter from the storm.

The snow was sliding down outside, as peaceful as thistledown. Mica crawled forward a little, then stopped to listen. Crawled forward some more. Froze, looking, listening, sniffing.

Nothing save the unhurried snow.

Mica put her head cautiously out of the opening. The valley and the hills were muffled in a pelt of thick white snow. The fluky wind was still whisking the snow into flurries, but there were no trails of footprints anywhere nearby.

So she had lived through the storm and she had escaped the howlmen. The howlmen were fierce and marvellous and strange, but she'd truly escaped them. She'd seen the stars in their calling, and—

'*Mica!*'

The voice was deadened by the snow, but it wasn't very far away.

Oh, and that was Bear, kind, infuriating, stupid, pedestrian Bear, come to find her. To bring her safely home.

Home? But how could she go home?

But how could she *not* go home? She'd survived the blizzard, but—

'Mica! *Mica!*'

Mica could see him, now. He was labouring through the snow: looking, and hoping, and despairing, and looking again.

'Please, Mica!' he shouted. 'Mica, come back! I need you. Even the mad bits. You're right, Mica, I understand, now. I always did, really. Mica! Mica, *I need all of you!*'

But he didn't *know* all of her. Couldn't begin to imagine it. Especially now she'd moved along the patterns of the stars.

Mica looked down from the little mound where the wind had whirled the snow round and round and dropped it lightly over the corpse of a mammoth.

Then, cringing with guilt, she backed quietly back inside it again, out of sight.

Chapter 44

It was a long while before Mica could be sure that Bear was right out of sight, and by then there were black dots like gnats spinning in front of her eyes.

That was because she was hungry, of course. She might have seen the patterns of the stars, but she hadn't eaten since yesterday. She needed food.

She crawled out of the mound, forced her stiff limbs to straighten, and then turned and made her way down the slope.

The remains of the wind was whisking the snow into scurrying drifts, but she trudged on doggedly until specks appeared in front of her eyes that she couldn't blink away.

What were they, so far away on the other side of the snowy river?

Hyenas? A herd of elk?

No.

No.

Those were stonemen.

Mica stopped short.

That was Seal and Amber and Garnet down there.

All the stonemen who could hunt except for Bear, who was searching for her.

So few. It had never really struck Mica before, but there were so very very few of them.

They were cutting up some beast to carry home. They'd managed to kill something at last, then, or else they'd found some poor creature frozen to death in the blizzard. There were two big hunks of meat laid ready on the ground behind them. Yes, Seal was loading up the women with meat, and now he was hoisting up a great joint himself, settling it across his mighty shoulders and then turning to lead the way back to the shelter.

Yes, that was right, that was the way home. She knew exactly where she was, now.

Mica waited until the stonemen were safely on their way, and then she walked down the slope towards the place where they'd killed. The stonemen were unlikely to have been able to carry the whole carcass home between three of them.

The snow was deep and clinging, and it wasn't long before the dots of hunger came back to fly clumsily before her eyes, lurching and spinning and . . .

. . . she had to stop or she might have fainted: and if she fainted she was going to freeze to death.

Mica blinked her vision clear and trudged on again. Soon she heard running water and discovered she was parched. Yes, here was the river. It was faster here than it was along by the shelter, and it wasn't yet quite frozen. Some large animal—an aurochs, or a great woolly rhino, perhaps—had crashed its way across the river this morning, and amidst the tinkling of the hurrying water there were fragments of ice bumping and rocking along, sometimes joining each other to form new islands before being forced apart again.

Mica looked along the river. Seal and the others were still not very far away. If she shouted they would probably hear her: and then she would soon be warm and fed again.

Mica drank, squatting down, watching the dizzy rocking of the pieces of ice.

And did not call to them.

Chapter 45

It wasn't easy for Mica to summon up the energy to move on from the river. She was tired, and it was hard to move her eyes away from the chunks of ice clinking and swirling in all the tiny currents of the river. Two spinning pieces of ice caught each other—held together for a moment—and then spun apart.

They dipped round and under each other, each trail separate and yet part of all the others.

Round and round and going nowhere.

Chink, tap, chlunk.

No sense. No rest. Going nowhere.

Some people could live their lives like these chunks of ice, pushed round and round in the currents of hunger and cold, unable even to imagine a way out to any sort of freedom: but Mica couldn't live in that sort of blundering blindness. Her life had to be an active thing: constantly watchful, constantly searching, looking for echoes, for patterns, for new worlds.

She got up, and soon her feet were throbbing with the pain of the blood pounding back into them.

Those howlmen had understood about living.

Their calls, the way they'd moved round the fire, the little reindeer, they had all been steps into other worlds. Places completely new. Oh, and there were a multitude of worlds in the valley, all overlapping: a reindeer world, a bear world, even a star world.

What might be in them? What wonders might there be to discover?

Mica made her way across to the place where Seal and Amber and Garnet had been cutting up their prey. There were tracks leading back towards the shelter, but Mica hardly looked at them.

The beast had been a young horse, far too skinny to have survived the winter, but all the same too much for the stonemen to carry home. They had left the head behind.

There was enough meat on it to keep Mica going for another day.

Mica walked along the river bank, and soon the gushing, pirouetting water narrowed to a trickle, and soon after that the ice closed its fist and winter held the whole thing fast.

She was walking because otherwise all she could do was sit in the snow.

She hesitated at the track that led up to the shelter. She heard voices for a moment, lifted on a gust of wind, and she wavered.

Amber would miss her. Elk would, too. And young Lynx.

I need you, even the mad bits, Bear had said.

And yet . . .

And yet she couldn't stay with the stonemen. Staying meant killing most of what made her herself.

I have seen the patterns of the stars, she whispered.

But then she looked up at the dull white sky. And she realized that the stars were still far, far beyond her reach, and even further still beyond her understanding.

In the end Mica turned up the track that led back to the shelter of the stonemen.

Chapter 46

Mica could hear the stonemen's voices long before she reached the edge of the clearing. Bear's voice was amongst them. He must have given up looking for her and come home.

(But of course he had. Looking for one person in all this snow was hopeless. Of course he'd given up.)

'How did you catch it?' Elk was asking.

What? But of course, they were talking about the horse. Not about her at all.

'Seal brought it down.' That was Garnet, full of pride and triumph. 'We came up behind the herd and shouted, and Seal was waiting for them. He jumped on it and slit its throat.'

A grunt from Seal.

'It carried me a long way,' he said. 'It scraped my skin half off.'

'But you got it in the end,' said Elk, happily.

'Well, I wasn't letting it get away, I can tell you. We'll eat fresh meat tonight.'

There was a pause, and then Bear said:

'And what will we eat tomorrow, Strongest?'

'Oh, there's food enough for days, here,' said Elk. 'Look at this! A whole rind of fat, eh? Makes your mouth water just to look at it.'

Mica listened.

'Well, what about next moon, then?' asked Bear, just a little impatient. 'What about midwinter? Nearly all the beasts will be gone from the valley by then. And even you, Strongest, won't be bringing down a mammoth or a rhino with your bare hands.'

'We've got all that meat pickling in the pool,' said Garnet, quickly. 'That'll feed us for moons. And there'll be bulrush roots.'

'I won't survive this winter, anyway,' said Pearl's voice, querulously. 'You'll be supping *my* meat before spring. Eh, but I bet I'll be tough!'

Then Amber said:

'What are you doing, Bear?'

'This hide is mine,' said Bear. 'I'll need it tonight if I can't find any other shelter. You won't need it if I'm gone.'

A second's silence.

'Bear—' began Elk.

'And I'll need some food,' went on Bear. 'Don't worry, I'll not take much, but I've worked and hunted for you for all these years so I'm due something. Just a piece of that horse will do, to keep me going for a day or so.'

'Bear,' said Amber, quietly. 'We all miss Mica very much, but we're hoping she'll come back soon, safe and sound. She probably found somewhere to shelter last night, and—'

'No,' said Bear, and Mica, listening to him, could imagine the shake of his head as he said it. 'Mica's not coming back. She doesn't *want* to come back. You know that.'

'We'll be better off without her, anyway,' muttered Garnet, sourly. 'Her head's full of things that aren't there. Full of the wind. And it isn't blowing from the sunny side, either.'

'Mica is young,' said Amber, turning on her swiftly. 'And young ones are not always wise.'

Seal let out a bark of scorn.

'Young ones are not *ever* wise,' he said. 'They speak when they should be silent, and think things that are best not thought.'

'Then you won't miss me,' said Bear.

Elk spoke quickly.

'Oh, no, you are valuable to us, Bear. We wish you to stay.'

'No you don't,' said Bear, promptly. 'You wish me to live. I can't tell you how grateful I am to you and Amber for finding me, and for looking after me as I grew up. But I can manage by myself, now. And you don't want Mica here, either. Not really. Now she's left you've got some hope for her.'

'Hope?' echoed Amber, in a voice full of pain; but Elk cleared his throat.

'Mica is stronger than she looks, wife,' he said. 'I've always said that. She's not one to sit down and die. No, she's always been awkward, that one. A fighter.'

'I know,' said Bear. 'And that's why she's not coming

back. She doesn't want to die, not in her body or her mind. And neither do I, and so I've realized I've got to be a fighter, too. And that means I've got to fight my way out of the old ways and find new ones, to suit these new times that have come.'

'But if you leave, how will Mica know where to find you?' asked Pearl, craftily. 'For wherever she's gone, she may return.'

Bear made no reply, but Mica could hear the sounds of movement, of the hefting of a burden.

'Can I come?' asked Lynx, as if it was the most important thing in the world.

'Not this time,' said Bear, gently. 'You must stay here and learn lots. Learn as much as you can.'

'But where will you go, Bear?' asked Amber.

Mica could hear that Bear had already turned away when he replied.

'Into the future,' he said.

Chapter 47

Mica stayed hidden until Bear had walked past her down the track. Then she waited a little longer.

Part of her was shouting *hurry hurry, or you'll never be able to catch up with him!* and part of her was whispering *hide, hide. He'll never let you be free if he finds you.*

But at last she slipped out from behind a snow-clotted clump of grass and turned down the track after him.

Bear's tracks cut cleanly through the frozen crust of the snow, and Mica walked in his footsteps so that the stonemen would never know that she had been watching them.

It was possible that the stonemen would survive the winter without her and Bear. Without them, the great mass of mammoth meat pickling in the pond would last much longer. Perhaps the stonemen might survive. Pearl was getting thinner and thinner and she'd surely be dead by midwinter. And the fewer of them there were, the better their chances would be.

Mica reached the river and turned along it.

She followed Bear's tracks across the pool, through

the broken reeds, and onto the path. From that point there were several sets of footprints coming and going through the snow, and it was easy to follow the tracks that led up towards the shelter of the howlmen.

She toiled up the slope to the ridge. She was surprised she couldn't see the howlmen's camp from there, but perhaps the contours of the valley were hiding it.

The snow had finally twisted to a halt, now, and the whole valley was possessed of a huge stillness that was broken only by her panting breath and the creaking of the snow under her feet.

She'd walked so far now that she would have thought she'd got lost if it hadn't been for the tracks. Where was the howlmen's shelter?

And then the tracks ended. There was a discoloured patch that must have been the site of the fire, but all the rest was gone. Quite gone. All that was left was a wide trail of swept snow as if something huge had been dragged away along the bottom of the valley.

Mica could hardly believe it. The fierce, marvellous, extraordinary howlmen had gone, gone right away like the beasts to follow the sun.

Mica stepped into the circle that had held the howlmen's fire and that had been the centre of their calling. She squatted down and put her hand on the ground as if in the hope of absorbing some of the howlmen's knowledge from the frozen soil.

It was there that Bear found her. She recognized his footsteps long before she looked up.

'They've gone,' she said.

Bear came and squatted down in front of her.

'They would have killed you, Mica,' he said.

She knew that was true. Or almost-knew it.

'But how can I live?' she said. 'I can't go back. I need . . . I need . . .'

'Marvels,' said Bear, steadily. 'A new world.'

'But I can't reach one!' said Mica; and suddenly she began to cry.

Bear took hold of her hands.

'But one day you will,' he said urgently. '*We* will. Yes, we *will*, Mica.'

But she couldn't believe it.

'I watched them,' she said. 'The howlmen. I heard them calling, and I saw them move round their hearth. I even saw the stars in their voices. But I still don't . . . it's still not part of me.'

Bear blinked.

'But of course it's not,' he said. 'Watching's not enough.'

'But . . .'

'Watching . . . that's just like you showing me all your thoughts,' he said earnestly. 'It's no good unless you can find a way to catch hold of them. To join hands with them.'

Bear's own hands were warm.

'But how can I catch hold of the stars?' she cried in frustration.

'I don't know,' he said at once. 'Most likely you never will. But there's all sorts of things we *can* catch hold of, Mica. And we can build a whole world of them. Our own world.'

'But I can't! I *can't*. I can't make things work. My hunting thing kept falling to pieces, Bear. You saw that for yourself. It just wouldn't *work*!'

But Bear's eyes were alight with eagerness.

'It will if you wet the thongs before you tie them on,' he said. 'The thongs will shrink as they dry, then, and they'll get so tight round the pebbles they'll *never* come off.'

Mica's mouth fell open. Bear was right. If they soaked the thongs . . .

'But . . . how did you know that?' she asked, really shocked.

He shrugged.

'I don't know,' he said. 'I suppose you were letting your idea go and I . . . well, I just caught hold of it. I wanted to help you.'

Bear suddenly got up and shrugged off the bundle he was carrying on his back. He was talking fast, his words falling over one another in his eagerness.

'Look, I have a pelt to shelter us,' he said. 'And food for today, and perhaps for tomorrow, as well. So we can do it, Mica. We can make our own world. Just think of the marvels it'll have in it. Look, here is the first of them.'

He brought out something from the folds of his furs. It was a little ivory figure which would some day be a bear.

Mica closed her hands round its warmth.

And then she looked up at the sky again, which would surely always be far out of her reach. But perhaps, just perhaps, she might begin to make a whole trail of ideas that would get to the stars one day, even if she never lived to see it herself.

'We can do it, Mica,' said Bear. 'It's all right. I *know* we can.'

Bear's eyes were glowing, and she suddenly realized there was enough warmth in them to keep her living for many a day.

Mica nodded. She wiped her face and got to her feet, and took his hand in hers.

And then together they turned, and began to make their way up towards the far arches of the hills.

Prehistorical Note

Mica's adventures take place about forty thousand years ago, at the beginning of the last Ice Age. Evidence of Neanderthal life in what we now call Britain is scanty, but we know that Neanderthals and our own species, Homo sapiens, did meet each other at some point, as Svante Pääbo's work on Neanderthal DNA has shown that all the people of the Earth, except for sub-Saharan Africans, have at least one Neanderthal ancestor.

I read a lot about Neanderthals when I was planning this book, and I ended up very confused indeed. My special thanks are due to Mark J. White of the University of Durham who very kindly sent me his marvellous paper *Things To Do In Doggerland When You're Dead*, which made everything much clearer.

Dan Fisher of the University of Michigan was the brave man who proved, by eating it, that chunks of meat thrown into a pond get naturally pickled by lactobacilli.

Neither of these fine clever men, though, is even slightly to blame for my wild imagination, which I drew upon to construct this story, nor for any errors of fact in this book.

Turn the page
to discover more
captivating books
from Oxford ...

Cold Tom

'One of those rare, strange, wonderful books that
makes you see the world through different eyes'
Guardian

'The finest first novel I've read since David
Almond's *Skellig*' *Glasgow Herald*

'enthralling and original' *Bookseller*

'outstanding' *Sunday Times*

Ice Maiden

THE STUNNING SEQUEL TO *COLD TOM*

'startling, suspenseful and ultimately very satisfying' *The Times*

'written with a beautiful clarity' *The Bookbag*

'a marvellously woven tale of nature versus civilisation' *Wordpress.com*

Coming in February 2013

The performances at The Royal Theatre are extraordinary. You'd have to see them to believe them! But that's the problem. Nobody can see them. Except Gracie, that is.

Gracie's new to this seaside town, but she's making friends quickly. There's Mikey the Mod who wears a parka and drives a scooter, Miss Melluish whose skirt is missing, and Frank Stuart, the builder of elephants.

But the old theatre is under threat. Will Gracie and the residents be able to save their home, or is the curtain set to fall on their very last performance?

'EVERYBODY SHOULD READ
GERALDINE MCCAUGHREAN'
Philip Reeve

Coming in April 2013

What if you woke up tomorrow and everything had changed?

Money is worthless.

Your friends are gone.

Armed robbers roam the streets.

No one is safe.

For Matt and his little brother, Taco, that nightmare is a reality. Their only hope of survival is to escape through the Channel Tunnel. But danger waits on the other side…

Stay or go. What would *you* do?

AN UNFLINCHINGLY POWERFUL NOVEL FROM THE WINNER OF THE CARNEGIE MEDAL